Santo Gordo
A Killing in Oaxaca

Charles Kerns

For Roshni who took me to Oaxaca
and other wonderful places

CONTENTS

With thanks to Mama and Luz
and all the people of Oaxaca
who welcomed me to their city

Churro

Christ, it's beautiful.

I looked up at the yellow flowering trees in the courtyard and then walked into the market planning to take a shortcut out of the late summer heat. It was cooler inside and I could hit the bakery stalls and get a second breakfast. I always went into these *mercados*, not the supermarket knockoffs they started building in the malls down here. The real thing had four walls enclosing about an acre, with a sheet metal roof over dozens of simple stalls, maybe ten by ten feet. Each one had food piled too high to reach, apples, oranges, vegetables, meat–they refrigerate it now–dead plucked chickens lined up, five foot stacks of thin sliced beef, and local cheeses–string balls or drippy creams right from a farm down the road. And then there were the chocolates and hand-made candies. I loved it.

I wandered through, entered the aisle of bakeries and bought myself a *churro* covered with chocolate. I forced myself out the far side of the market, started sweating again from the heat and walked the half block over to Avenida Morales. My straw sombrero helped a little. It kept the sun off my head, but it also kept the heat and sweat in, except for the dribbles running behind my ears. But I would be out of the sun soon. That was what I thought.

The street was not crowded, only a sedan and a bus were there. I guessed everyone had turned off because of the strikers' blockade. Or maybe the cops were stopping cars from coming this way.

As I stepped out in the street, a big Mercedes sports convertible sped around the corner and forced me back to the curb. Some big shot sat behind the wheel with a boy beside him. The top was down and I could see the man wore a fancy suit and shades like a movie star.

I was about to yell at him for cutting me off when a couple crazy little motorcycles zoomed up the wrong side of the street. Two riders sat on each one of these *motos*—that's pretty normal here. Sometimes they have five on a bike if you count the infants. I watched their backs as they pulled on black ski masks. That was not normal.

They cut in front of the Mercedes. It swerved and crunched a fender into the stone wall. One man slid off the back of each *moto* and ran at the car. The *moto* drivers stopped, planted their feet and kept the engines whining.

The big shot in the Mercedes leaned forward and started to yell at the two in front. Then he reached quickly someplace down below the dashboard. The guys with masks pulled out some big looking guns. I threw myself on the ground thinking this is crazy. My *churro* flew into a puddle and I thought what a waste.

I didn't see the rest, but I heard the pops and the glass breaking. The *motos* revved up and took off. The boy in the car started screaming.

I looked up. People were edging back on the sidewalk, hiding behind the doors in the walls. Slamming them shut. A couple was driving off fast in their beat-up sedan holding down kids in the back seat. The bus lumbered on, not noticing anything.

No more guns, I hoped. I waited. The boy started yelling, "Papi, Papi." I stood up and walked to the car. The windshield had small punched-in circles with crazed glass edges right in front of the driver and, just like in the newspaper's *Sección Roja*, the guy was flopped back with his sunglasses falling to the side, blood oozing down. The boy was shaking. I grabbed the door, pulled it open and reached in. I got my arms around him. He held on to the man and was bloody. I squeezed him tight and smothered him with my arms. He beat on me yelling and then started crying big sobs. I didn't know if he was shot. I looked in the car and the guy had some kind of gun by his hand. I thought he was dead but I took off with the kid, turning the street corner to get out of sight.

The boy seemed like he had not been hit. He was squirming hard and starting to yell again. I just took a deep breath and said *conserva la calma* like the earthquake and disaster posters everywhere down here told me to do. I hugged the boy harder and hoped the Virgin–the one my landlady was always praying to—was working overtime, protecting us both.

Espresso

I woke early that morning. I should have slept in and been late for the murder, but it was just too damned beautiful.

I leaned back and looked out over my balcony at the purple bougainvillea covering the neighbor's wall, not hanging down so much as enveloping the side of the building. For all I knew, it held that eroded adobe wall from full collapse. Tourists took its picture every day. The Policía cordoned it off with yellow plastic crime tape a while back.

"It's going to fall some day," they explained. "But it´s not a crime. The wall is three hundred years old and it is owned by–who knows?"

Now the tape was lying in the gutter. Kids pulled it down yesterday and ran around with it streaming behind them. *Cuidado*–be careful–was printed all down the tape and easy to read even from across the street.

You needed warnings here in Oaxaca. The sidewalks were cracked and uneven. Never flat. They had tank-trap manholes, their covers stolen or broken into cement powder by the overloaded trucks cutting corners on roads meant for burro carts and now filled with big rigs. Trees roots, semis and washed out sewers tilted the concrete slabs and made walking a balancing test that you failed a couple times a week.

In front of the bougainvillea, two frayed wires trailed from an improvised splice at the base of a street lamp still shining into the morning shadows. The wires snaked down the street through muddy puddles to some slapped-together stalls selling pirate CDs and tee shirts silkscreened with Che, Subcomandante Marcos and the Virgin of Guadalupe. Children stomped through the puddles bare footed, laughing, loved as only Mexican children can be.

Everyone coming south from el Norte to stay in Oaxaca was careful for their first months, walking, eating, driving, drinking. But then they grew used to the dangers and dropped the mindfulness that strange geography brings. That was when bad things happened.

Don't be afraid, though. It could be heaven here. Everyone told me so. Warm, sunny, friendly, and cheap. And freedom-filled if you were too dumb to know better– the way most expats lived. Like long-term tourists, boxed in, guarded in the hotel zone with their hot showers, working toilets and spiced cooking.

I finally got up, dressed and headed out before the sun cleared the two-story, solid earth walls that edged the streets, forming the city's long straight corridors. Those walls locked most gringos out of the real life taking place in big family courtyards, behind closed doors. They could hear it: kids yelled as they chased each other inside. They could smell it: foods were grilling and simmering all the time. And they could glimpse through the metal gates as people came and went: aunts, cousins, grandmothers and school children in their sweaters and uniforms.

Then the gates slammed shut. You were closed out, thankfully not alone on the street most of the time. But late at night, after a mezcal or two, with street lights flickering and making deep doorway shadows, you looked over your shoulder and wondered about the sirens a couple blocks away.

Don't get chased down these streets at night—no shelter can be found when the metal doors and the windows with wrought iron grills are locked tight and bolted.

And don't walk the streets after the sun gets high either. Only tourists do. The noon sun was more than hot—you thought it drove darts in your skin, like the arrows that made the gilded saints in the cathedral into martyrs.

I lived near the Centro, the tourist area. It was easier living there. The Mexicans kept it like a dream for short time visitors from el Norte: it had colors, music, weavings, hotels, and pedestrian-only walkways. They didn't want to run over their gringos, like they did the dogs and bicyclists that you saw in the *Sección Roja*—that was the "red" section of the local newspaper. Red, blood red, always with close ups of bodies laid out for the camera by the local cops getting their small payout from the photographer. It was easy to skip that section if you only had a couple days in a four-star, but was harder to miss if you lived here permanently with the pictures always hanging in front of you in all the newspaper stalls.

I climbed down the concrete steps and passed the flower-covered altar to one of the local Virgins–the Lady of Lost Hopes, I called her. My landlady, Señora Concepción, had added enough fresh flowers to keep this Virgin Mary happy and praying for us all day long.

I was lucky. I lived over a family courtyard in a little apartment. I stayed away from the housing mazes stuffed with tourists in high season and mostly empty the rest of the year. In my place, I got to see and hear a bit of family life, the real Oaxaca. Señora Concepción's son Jorge, his wife Victoria and three children lived scattered in rooms around the house´s open courtyard with its ancient stone fountain, ropey vines climbing the walls, lizards sunning themselves, the morning laundry strung from tree to stairs, chickens hiding behind the laundry, and the family sedan being washed again.

I walked by the fountain, called out *hola* to Jorge scrubbing the car's tires and went through the metal doors out to the wall-lined street. It was hard for most tourists to imagine the life locked in these courtyards. They had hints from the crazed growth of vines that crept out over the walls. Mostly flowers, but lurking in the leaves were cactuses to let you know what waited if you tried to climb in. Their spines warned everyone of the more dangerous glass shards embedded in the top of the adobe walls, near the barbed wire that was a last protection from the street. We prayed these old defensive habits of Mexican homeowners were no longer needed, but memories of hiding from guns and bandits and revolutions took a long time to die.

I hugged the shade by the wall, jumped the open manhole in the sidewalk near my house's front door and walked a couple blocks to the Llano Park. I passed the two cement lions guarding the park entrance while they nursed the stubs of their tails, always recently repaired but then snapped off by young men establishing their bragging rights late in the night. At least that was what I figured happened.

I crossed the park's two-block width of grass now browning in the heat, so carefully swept each morning by workers pushing their tree-branch brooms. I followed the shadows of the hundred-foot trees through the park's central plaza and then, reaching the other side, cut between two wildly painted cargo trucks, covered with virgins and devils, and crossed the traffic-clogged street.

I pushed the door open at La Avenida, my morning espresso stop. The barista stood sharply dressed, attentive and smiling. Starbucks got locked out of the Centro by the lefty politicos, but Starbuck culture seeped in. Espresso bars were everywhere, even where tourists never went, in the middle class and rich parts of town. But they said old native chocolate, hand-mixed into a frothy, hot morning drink, still ruled in the barrio south of the Centro, where the low paid workers and those always looking for work lived.

Charles called to me. "You're early." He had been sitting, waiting for one of us expats to come in. I was known for my late appearance. The others must have had a long night drinking because they usually beat me here.

He was tall, on the edge of portly; his scant pony tail pulled tight, hanging past the collar on his guayabera shirt. I called him a Type One. Type Twos were the rich Texans up the hill, flying in and out, living the gated-community life. Type Ones were like me, living almost Mexican, pulling social security, maybe something on the side, not much, but enough if you're careful.

Charles made and lost his money doing startups. He still had his lawyerly, hustling habits, trying to put together some kind of deal but was way past his prime. He usually slept in late, ate fancy, and got a little high on the rooftop terrace every couple nights with a couple of other Type Ones.

Type One women came up on the terrace too, a bit younger–artists, poets, photographers–with hippie names like Fawn and Rainbow. They had grown kids back in the States and looked tired when they got here. You had the feeling they started life too young or maybe went too fast. Sometimes they paired up with the men; sometimes they brought ones with them. Who knows where their money came from? Every so often, one talked a restaurant or bar into holding a show, hanging her photos or prints on the walls to make a couple dollars selling to tourists. Type One women wrote in their journals, painted watercolors, took photos of the women and children on the streets and cooked a lot in their rooms. They were busier than the men.

A lot of Type Ones, men, women and couples, just did winters, give or take a little, here in Oaxaca. The part-timers showed up on the rooftop, too. They were not on vacation; they lived here like the rest of us, knew everyone, knew their shops and street vendors, and resumed their well-worn routines after the flight or bus ride in. These Type Ones just lived in other places too, in a complicated, on-going clockwork of different friends and cities. They migrated, like some of the high flying birds down here, to the warm, friendly-to-American places of the world.

Sometimes I joined the rooftop where the Type Ones watched the stars in the evening, talking their sometimes-hopeful, sometimes-desperate, but never very active, politics and recounting the search for good doctors, miracle stomach meds and mezcal dealers. Some Type One men used their nights checking out new women arrivals, to see what they might be interested in. Some just leaned back and sipped mezcal, watching the sky and taking it in. Some did not sip; they drank hard and rambled through the night, even after the others had left.

Usually I stayed home though, went to sleep early, read mystery novels and studied my Spanish verbs. Beyond that, I had a couple Mexican friends I drank with on weekends when they were off work. Getting past the northern invader relationship with them was hard, but after a couple of years it was starting to happen. Those friends did not meet on the roof with the Type Ones. The expats' roof had become a gringo-only zone. Their little, down-at-the-heels American outpost was for cheerleading fellow gringos, not for mixing with the locals.

Charles gave me a big Mexican hug, the type Mexicans do, with a couple back slaps. He was back from the States on one of the cheap red-eyes, and about to pop with news, way too much for me before coffee. I tried to get away, headed up to the counter but he had no one else to tell, so he followed me,

"*Cortado doble.*" I called. The barista nodded, clamping the coffee canister to his impressive machine, looking like a leftover from the steam train era.

"Did you see the black 737s fly in? They taxied up right beside us when we landed this morning and the Federales all marched out in riot gear."

Dark liquid was dripping quickly into the small cup. I watched as the drops slowed.

"You know the government bought up a bunch of forty-year-old jetliners for the army and painted them black, with a gold eagle on the tail. When the Federales got out of the plane today, coming down those roll-up ramps, they all had tall, see-through shields and batons with handles and were dressed like a motorcycle gang playing Darth Vader."

I nodded. I figured he had practiced that line in his head waiting for someone to come along. He still had a long way to go with the story. The barista steamed some milk and scooped a spoon of foam on the espresso. It was ready. I don´t sip it like Italians. I took a mouthful, trying to cool it with the foam. I needed the jolt to get going.

"They climbed into buses out on the runway. Black buses. And get this. They put those big plastic shields blocking the window. I know it's hot that way but no bricks or stones are coming through when they drive down the streets."

I looked out the window. Late summer winds blew through the trees in the park. Children played soccer on the pavement in front of the closest fountain. A couple skateboarders jumped the old carved stone seats that dated back to when no Indians were allowed in the park.

"You know where they were heading, over to the *plantón*–the strike. Those teachers wanting more money won't leave; they will sit in front of the municipal office forever. They have tents and are cooking and even took the port-a-potties that the government brought in for the dance festival. Something is going to happen soon."

"You know the teachers strike every year," I said.

"Yeah, but remember when they trashed the city."

I wasn't sure if he thought the police or the teachers trashed the city. Maybe both. It happened a couple years back and the city was still recovering. I watched it all back then. The old Governor ran the teachers out of town with the army. Now the old Governor was gone–a new one had been elected this year–and the teachers never really left.

"Are you heading out today? Remember they might do something."

I thought the strikers and police would keep far enough apart so that they could only eye each other. The tourists would stay away from that part of the city. But I needed to head over there later.

"Another *cortado*, single this time." I needed more caffeine to get going. "And a *cuernito*–a croissant." They were like big, rolled biscuits down here, probably loaded with lard, but they dunked well and left an oily rainbow sheen on the surface that you could stare at until the caffeine kicked in.

"Well, we'll see. Just have to wait," I responded slowly.

Then Charles saw Lark, one of the local Type A gringas, when she walked in. He looked for a way to end our conversation and get over to her with his story. She liked to talk politics. She was one of those progressives, that was what she called it, who said she was staying till Bush Junior was out, but I think she is here for good. A good match for Charles, I mean Carlos. I have to remember, last week he announced he was now Carlos. Like the King of Spain.

That happens to us down here. Our names get Spanished. Like mine got an "o" on the end after a year or so. Now Roberto sounds more like me than old Robert ever did.

"Well have a good day." I helped Carlos end our talk. He nodded and headed to Lark´s table. I needed to start thinking about how to get over to the other side of town through the blockades.

I know the idea of blockades by strikers sounds bad, but they are like our war demonstrations up north where everyone, the strikers and the cops, know what is supposed to happen. In the States some volunteer to get arrested. Here everyone stays out of jail if they can help it.

The striking teachers screw up traffic. They commandeer a bus or two. The bus drivers take the strikers where they want to go. They order the bus to the big intersections and block the lanes. Everyone in town has to drive slow detours around them. I hated the traffic detoured in front of my house, going two miles an hour, with diesel exhaust and gas fumes filling the street. If this were the States I would be suing them for my never-ending cough.

The bus drivers and strikers wait until comida—that is dinner—about 4 PM. The strikers let the buses leave. And the bus company pays the drivers for their day and to bring the buses back. The drivers continue their routes, like nothing happened, picking up passengers along the way. And the traffic cops stay away. And the crime cops pretend like it's the traffic cops' job. It's just those Federales, the national police that fly around in jets. They will mess up this game one day.

I decided to walk over to the bank first. I was out of money and needed a transfusion from the States. It was already hot but I was lucky the sun was still not quite up over the walls and the shade was dark and deep if you stayed close to the adobe.

I had to pay bills today. Credit cards didn't work here for basic things like electricity and internet in your apartment. Everyone Mexican waited until the last day of the month and then queued for a couple hours to pay. I wanted to be my old prompt all-American self, but I had absorbed the ways down here too deeply and lost my old on-time habits.

I needed to cut over to Avenida Morales. I walked quickly for two blocks through the Centro, circling around the day's almost stationary cars and trucks. It was crowded. All traffic went through the center of town. Buses and trucks heading up for Mexico City normally just plowed through. Today, the blockades had them trapped. It reminded me of back before freeways in the States, when I was a kid. You had all the signs for the routes on every downtown corner. The truck routes ran through the poor parts of Baltimore where I grew up, sort of like a maze, and you won if you made it out of the city. Then the freeways came and cut the city into slices that let the trucks out and trapped us kids if we were not careful.

Down here in Oaxaca there was no freeway. Just old streets that dated back to right after Cortéz, now carrying more traffic in a day than they did in their first hundred years. If you didn't count the soldiers marching through back then.

I reached a little plaza in front of one of the city's mercados and looked up at the yellow flowers. I went in to the market, bought a *churro* and cooled off as I got out of the sun and walked through the food stalls.

Then it happened. I walked out. The Mercedes came at me; the *motos* zoomed up and shot through the windshield. The dead man slumped and the boy yelled.

My Oaxaca ended.

I got the boy and held him still. Then two traffic monitors, sort of, but not-quite cops, came running toward the car. One turned to me. I handed her the boy. The other started yelling for more cops. They started arriving fast. Real cops with guns and rifles and radios. Two to a motorcycle. Big leather boots. Sirens. And then a helicopter. This dead guy must have been important. This was serious.

I sat on the sidewalk corner. I felt sticky from the blood on the boy. It got on my shoes, my hands, my shirt. The boy was quiet now and riding off in a police car. I sat still. One policeman stood in front of me. I knew I was not going anywhere for a while.

Mole

"Roberto, are you all right?"

Arturo, my Mexican friend, was sitting in front of me at a sidewalk table in the Zocalo, the city's main square, looking at me like you would some science specimen to see if it was still alive, maybe wanting to poke it to see if it moved.

"I think so. It was crazy."

I had called Arturo just after I left the police station. I was in there three hours. The captain, in full uniform, even wearing his army-style hat pulled down tight, sweating hard, kept asking me the same questions "Why were you there? Who was shooting? What happened on the street? Why were you there?"

My answers were simple. Bad luck. Don't know. Didn't see anything. And then, Bad luck, again.

Then they told me to go. I went home, tried to avoid the Señora, scrubbed, put on a clean shirt, threw out the old one, pants too, and called Arturo. I needed to talk about it. He said to meet in the Zocalo and when he showed up on time, I knew he was worried. Time is pretty flexible down here and only the gringos think much about starting on the dot. Arturo normally gave me time to enjoy the day before he got there. That was how I explained it to myself. Everyone was interested in what you did when you got there, not when you arrived.

"We heard you were there. You saved the boy." Arturo stared at me when he talked.

"I didn't do anything. I just held him while his father died. And handed him to the police."

"Well everyone says an old gringo saved the boy. White beard. Short hair. And gordo like you. That's what everyone is saying."

I do not like to think of myself as gordo—fat—but that is almost a compliment here. It means you live well and didn't come close to starving to death like the farmers up in the mountains, but I didn't have time to think about how they described me. I wanted to find out what was going on.

"Yes, it was me. Only I did not save anyone. I don't know anything."

I had called Arturo because he would be the one to know what really had happened. He worked for the state, a técnico, an engineer for water supplies. He heard everything and usually said nothing. At least outside the family, which I had slowly been joining these past years over meals and the endless parade of parties for birthdays, baptisms, first communions and quinceñeras. Not to mention the regular holiday meals for saint days, Easter and the month-long celebrations of Navidad—our stateside Christmas is a little side show compared to what goes on here when baby Jesus makes his big entrance.

"Did the teachers go crazy?" I asked. "What were they thinking when they shot him? The Federales will rip them apart."

Arturo leaned closer. "It wasn't the teachers that did it. It was the ex-Governor. And the dinosaurs."

Dinosaurs were what they called men like the ex-Governor. They used methods of the last century—bullets and bribes. Or maybe those are for every century, I don't know. His party had run Oaxaca for the past fifty years and finally lost an election. With all this globalization the dinosaurs should have gone extinct long ago, but they were still dangerous. We expats tried to not notice them and their methods but we knew. And sometimes saw, like I did in the street that morning.

"The one that got shot—he was an enforcer, a Colonel, internal security, not a good man." Arturo was almost whispering now. "He knew a lot. As you say, he knew where the bodies were buried, maybe literally. The ex-Governor is now out of office and does not want anyone remembering details from his past six years."

"You mean he knocked off his own guy?" I was talking too loud. Arturo looked around. He leaned back and took a drink of his beer. He motioned for me to drink as well.

"Let's talk about this later. Come to my house this evening. Now, are you OK? Really OK?"

"This never happens to me." I shook my head, not believing my morning.

"Let's eat. Enjoy the day. Be calm. You are still here. The dead man was bad. He is gone. Remember, we are alive and our food is ready."

Arturo had ordered mole for us both. The smell helped me not think of the body and the boy. I thought of mole. It was a reason to live.

Tourist foodies had found it too, and felt the same way. They put their slogan, "Mole, say it like olé!–a sauce to die for!" in the tourist brochures. I was a little jealous, like a lover who found his food had been unfaithful.

I did not care so much about the chicken that was with it but, oh, I fell in love again when I saw that thick brown mole sauce that started with chilies and chocolate ground together sometime yesterday and cooked and cooked until they poured it over my rice and brought it to the table. Yes, it was comida time and I saw Arturo's point. Be happy you are alive.

The waiter was on Arturo's side. He handed us two shots of mezcal–a liquor from the local agave plants, not Tequila, even better, from plants crushed, fermented and distilled on a farm right outside of town, with the clear liquid dripping from a coiled ancient copper tube, making almost pure alcohol, and the whole thing looking like it came from some hillbilly Ozark moonshine still.

Oaxaca was back-country too, far south of the sophisticated *Chilangos,* Mexico City people. Down here you had your family, your priest, your neighbors and maybe a friend that you watched out for, but you ducked out of the way when anyone from the other side of town had had troubles.

Arturo was right. It was time to eat and rest. And *conserva la calma*. We could talk later, in private.

He ate quickly and quietly. I got extra tortillas and sopped up the mole sauce. Life was good that afternoon. Except for the boy screaming in my head and my hands feeling sticky and it wasn't the mole that I felt.

Arturo finished. He looked at his watch. "I am sorry, Roberto, today is, as you said, crazy. The police are still swarming and they want us all back near our government offices. I know–water engineers–why them? We have to listen when something like this happens."

As if to help me understand, the police helicopter flew low over the Zocalo. Normally they did that to scare the strikers. Today it seemed to be heading somewhere. I shook Arturo's hand, thanked him and he headed back to the water commission office.

I still had some chicken on my plate. I cut the thigh into pieces, sopped them in the mole sauce and chewed each one slowly for a few minutes, counting the bites. Then drank a beer. I was feeling steadier. I had a couple hours before Arturo would go home and we could talk. And I still needed to go to the bank.

The bank was across the Zocalo. I used an ATM where lots of foot traffic surrounded the machine, where streetlights shone brightly if I went at night, and where I did not stand out much. That was a problem for a white bearded, short haired, pink-skinned, gordo gringo. I stuck out most of the time, but there were lots of us in the

Zocalo. And the ones in cargo pants and tee shirts or the flowery Hawaiian ones, carrying a camera or two, stuck out a lot more than me. I headed across the square.

The Zocalo´s square was surrounded by sidewalk cafes. The cathedral was in the north and the old city hall, now a museum, in the south. Tall laurel trees shaded everything. A band shell, looking like something Sousa played in, sat in the center where the state orchestra gave concerts on Thursdays and again on Sunday afternoons. I passed balloon sellers, cotton-candy girls, pop-cycle men with their push carts, and the marimba players lugging their three-man instrument, as they all progressed around the Zocalo trying to interest the tourists who wandered by. This Mexican market dance made local people enough to money to eat and let the tourists enjoy their vision of a smiling, musical, multicolored Mexico.

There were Mexican tourists here, too. Yes, maybe half the tourists were from Mexico, from cities up north of Oaxaca, and a lot from Europe, too. You could tell them. The Europeans would never wear tee shirts. They wore upscale with designer clothes and thick wallets, knowing their Euros were better than gold.

Everyone dressed better than us gringos. Even the poor Mexicans with their ironed tee-shirts and pants. Of course, theirs had silkscreened names of old rock concerts and forgotten football games printed across the front. The poor here bought used and unsold clothes from el Norte after everything was unbundled in the *mercados*. But, even these clothes had carefully pressed creases and no wrinkles, not like the casual, uncaring look most Americans proudly carried around.

I cut through the center of the square, walking quickly along with a group of busy local people skipping the main tourist action. I passed the shoeshine stands all filled with business and government men reading their newspapers and talking on cell phones.

This was the heart of the city and if you looked around you saw everyone: workers digging and cleaning, professionals reading legal papers and blueprints while they sipped coffee, local families taking their kids for a walk, some thieves and pickpockets in the corners, political protesters with big posters of Jose Stalin and Carlos Marx, street sellers with everything from monkey puppets to hand-woven blouses, and finally the tourists. It was not a faked Disneyland. It had real action. Maybe that was the reason I loved it.

The bank gave me my week's pesos and didn't eat my card. I said my prayer of thanks to the Virgin of ATMs, tucked away everything and left the glassed-in, solar cooked, banking booth. I slid my wallet down, snugged deep in my front pocket–I didn't think any pickpockets were on duty today, but made sure no one got ideas–and walked briskly back towards my apartment. I was almost feeling like this was just another day.

After I turned past the cathedral I stopped. Federales were lined up on one side of portable metal barricades just north of the Zocalo with striking teachers on the other side, but that was normal these days. This time the government, not the strikers, had set up the barricades to keep the teachers out of the Zocalo. The soldiers let only tourists in through a break in their new metal wall. It was easy for the soldiers, because none of the strikers was trying to get in. At least it seemed that way. I thought I could tell who was who. Teachers dressed poorer and had browner skin than the tourists from Mexico City. In any case, everything was quiet. The Federales were on their cell phones, probably talking to new Oaxacan girlfriends. Their helmets and shields were stacked and ordered in military rows. The strikers were eating comida and sitting on the ground. Like I said, just another normal day. I squeezed through the barricade, said, *buenos días* to the police and then good appetite, *buen provecho*, to the teachers.

I got back to my building and pulled out my key. I opened the small human-sized cutout entry in the bigger metal drive-through doors and ducked as I went through. I am not tall, but everything down here is sized a bit smaller than even me. I have learned not to bump my head most of the time, and I wear a hat with a big straw brim to stop the sun and cushion me as I try to remember to duck.

Señora Concepción was waiting, praying in front of the Virgin.

"Oh, it was so terrible. They killed him right in front of his boy. Can you believe it? In front of the boy."

She was speaking Spanish, way too fast for me. I was lucky though. She repeated the same thing over and over and after a couple times I understood.

"So terrible," I agreed. She apparently had not heard yet of the gordo gringo. Or maybe I was slimmer in her eyes, I don't know.

"It is one thing to assassinate a man but God will not forgive you if you kill a child."

I started to protest that the child lived and the father was evil; then remembered I was playing dumb.

"To kill in front of a boy is murdering the good part in him. To kill the father in front of the boy is murdering most of him. I hope his family can love the boy back to health, God willing."

"I will pray for the boy," I said. I meant it.

This was my way to end the conversation with the Señora. She was eighty and knew a lot about praying. I was happy she prayed for me and my gringo soul–she told me that she did it every day. I was a believer–I believed anything might help.

I used praying as my getaway from the Señora. Mention it and she would stop for a few quick Hail Marys, at the very least, and you could duck out. I went as fast as my lungs and heart would let me go up the steps to my apartment and just sat for a while, looking out the window. Remembering how simply everything started this morning. Just me, the sun, and the bougainvillea across the street.

Hot Chocolate

I napped a while. It was hot. Sweaty was ok but sticky kept reminding me of the shooting. So I got up and decided to walk to the church–the big one–Santo Domingo, a couple blocks away, and just sit in the dark interior and be still. Then about seven or so I would grab a cab and head over to Arturo's. I hadn't asked yet, but I wanted to know if I should be scared. I was the only witness. At least the only witness dumb enough to wait for the police, the only one who did not hide. I watched the assassins do their work.

I left, walking out the door, watching for holes in the sidewalk and looking over my shoulder. If the ex-Governor were involved, then cops could be working for him helping to get rid of bad memories. I had a bad memory of the morning and I was afraid they might want to erase it; then it would be me who made the *Sección Roja* in the newspaper with a couple holes in him.

The Policía were everywhere in the street, but they were everywhere all over the city by now. Anyway, I was not looking for the low level cops, the ones in uniform. The street cops were poor and not asked to join in high level corruption and murder, jut the daily small peso stuff. At least those were the rumors.

I didn't know exactly who I was watching for. Certainly, not the big tour group of French and Germans that pushed down the sidewalk towards me. They took pictures of each other smiling in front of the bougainvillea and then of the local candy lady walking by, balancing a big basket of pralines on her head, waving and smiling and trying to get a sale from the Europeans with their nose-in-the-air expressions showing they did not do street food.

Then someone took a picture of me. I saw the big lens aimed at my head.

What was that for? Was he a tourist? I lost the photographer in the crowd. The camera was aimed at me as I walked out. I was not imagining it.

I quickly tried to blend in, look French, like the ones around me, and huddled close to the tour guide who was pointing at the leaning wall and explaining how adobe aged, first in one language and then another. No one was paying attention. One couple was picking the bougainvillea's purple flowers. Another was much too close to the wall that was leaning their way, but no one cared. We bunched together and moved herd-like over towards the Santo Domingo Church.

I broke from my new tourist friends as we passed the entrance. An old Zapotec Indian woman squatted by the door, wrapped in a shawl that let more air in than it kept out, her hand extended towards me. I placed a couple peso coins in her fist and she blessed me as I passed. I was out for all the blessings I could get that day.

My eyes started adjusting to the dark when I got inside and I tried not to trip on the first row of pews. Turning back I could see through the doorway, maybe, two hundred people in the street, mostly tourists. Lots of shorts, tank tops and tattoos. Not likely clothing for an undercover cop following me around. I went deeper into the sanctuary.

I looked up. Massive stone columns arched overhead. This sturdy church wrapped itself around you. I sat in the front row on one of the plain pine benches. Its boards bent when I sat. I could understand that. I weighed about the same as four or five of the women around me, all kneeling, fixated on the Virgin over the altar.

I looked at the front wall behind the Virgin. It was gilded, a hundred feet tall and wide enough for the sides to be hidden in dimness. Saints stood in niches all up the wall. More looked down from the ceiling, mostly martyrs, helping us below, down on our knees, learning how to suffer. I looked at their eyes rolled back in their heads. These saints felt no pain because they joined the next world, even before they left this one. Not like the Colonel in the car this morning. Not like the bodies in the *Sección Roja*. The dead saints got a wall of gold, not a newspaper photo.

Their wall shimmered behind the light of dozens of prayed-over candles, left by the faithful. They had asked for help, like the martyrs. Like I had done. I got up and lit a candle for the boy. And another for me.

I was an altar boy back in Baltimore. We didn't light candles for the dead there. We were Protestants. No gold there, either. But I remembered that same peace from back then, when I got away from the school and just sat in the dark. Now the churches in Baltimore were all locked except on Sunday mornings and a lot were shut down for good and fenced off. No place to find stillness up there anymore. Maybe that was why I was here.

I rested an hour or so, listening to the soft steps up and down the aisle, the snapping of camera shutters and soft murmurs of the tourists. I left the world behind.

Then he tapped my shoulder.

"Roberto Evans, correcto? Un momento por favor? A coffee across the street?"

I was numbed by the quiet of the church and got up docilely and followed a large middle aged man, wearing a tailored suit, much too hot for the weather, out the door and over to the Coffee Company shop.

"Hot chocolate," he ordered, "made with water, the Oaxacan way."

"Café con leche." I said.

We climbed up to the empty balcony over the street. He sat down and I followed.

"I understand you were at the assassination?"

"No, I was just walking by. I was just taking a short cut by the market."

"Well, the local newspaper has your picture saving the boy. I am here to thank you from the family."

"I was just now praying for him in the church," I said, meaning it and knowing that was the Mexican thing to say and do.

"We want you to know our gratitude and here is something to show how we feel."

He laid an envelope on the table.

"Oh, no. I did not do anything"

"Please for the family." He paused for a minute. I was silent looking away from the envelope.

"One final thing, do not talk to the press. I know they are coming to see you. A photographer just took your picture as you left your home. Please, you will not meet him." He raised his voice when he reached the <u>not</u> in his request.

"I am not going to meet anyone." I did not even want to meet you, I was thinking.

So much for my powers of observation. Not only was one guy following me taking pictures but a second was following the first. But I was not meeting anyone from the press that was for sure. I was out of this mess. It was bad luck to see dead people, especially when they were being shot. I did not want to be involved. Like any sane person down here.

"Thank you. I am sure you understand." He stood and left.

There went my theory of only poor Oaxacans drinking hot chocolate. He did not look like the type to live down by the railroad tracks. He took his chocolate with him. He looked more like a guy the ex-Governor might have working for him. But I was not going to try to figure all this out.

The envelope was still on the table. I picked it up. I knew I would be tempted if I held on too long. I took it, headed back to the church and dropped it in slot in the poor box. I guess that is what they called it here. That was what we called it at home. I hope he saw me drop it off.

Even if I agreed with him not to talk to the press, I did not think I had made a contract with him—a deal with the devil. That was what they called the ex-Governor. I had picked up the money as he asked, but the church ended up with it. Then again, maybe it was a deal and the church guaranteed the devil's work. The church likes to do that sort of thing as a first act for us sinners. So we can really mess up this life, before we get to the last chapter, repent and the chorus sings Halleluiah.

Bells rang. Evening mass. It was time to go.

I started to look for a taxi. Now I really wanted to talk to Arturo.

Nothing coming on my side of the square. Usually cabs are going by, leading the traffic home.

Cars here are packed. Families pass by in their old sedans after a day of selling to the tourists or working in some government office. They fill their old Nissans and the few VW bugs still running with three in the front and, maybe, five or six, in the back seat. And a plastic Christ or Mary protecting them in a way we gringos can only dream about.

Then I saw the taxis. About a hundred were lined up on the other side of the square, topped with bouquets of flowers, tied with white ribbons and chains of blossoms circling their windshields and grills. Dozens of *taxistas*–taxi drivers–stood in front in the cars. A band started playing with lots of loud brass and bass drums.

Two paper maché *monos*–giant dancing puppets ten feet tall–came around the corner. One, a dark haired woman with pointed breasts protruding three or four feet from her wood-framed body, was dressed in a simple skirt and blouse. Her partner was a dapper Mexicano sporting a foot wide moustache and an oversized suit probably made out of three or four bed sheets. Two men inside the *monos* swirled and danced holding up the puppets and making their long, limp arms swing out in large circles. The giant puppet man and woman moved round and round each other and down the center of the street in front of the *taxistas* and their cabs. The procession had begun.

It was Día de los Taxistas. I had forgotten.

A life-sized wooden statue of their patron saint, St. Fiacre, looked down from a platform carried on the shoulders of a dozen taxistas. This saint also cured hemorrhoids and VD. I guess that was why the cab drivers needed him. To bless their cars. And do repair work on the sinners.

The procession headed out from the square. The cabs crept behind their saint, stopping traffic and reminding everyone sitting, sweating in their cars that having a fiesta was more important than work or even getting home on time.

I watched as the taxi drivers threw candies out their car windows while they inched forward and children appeared from nowhere and ran into the street to grab their prizes.

This meant no taxi for me. The *taxistas* still had to go to church and be blessed and sprinkled with holy water. That was going take a long time.

I needed to take a bus. Not a bad way to travel if you are a bit smaller, but a squeeze for me. Arturo would be home soon and he was my best source of information, so I wanted to get there. Maybe even more important, he was my friend and would tell me what to do.

On the corner in front of the farmacia, buses were heading south, down towards the workers' barrios. All had hand-painted destinations on the windshield. Most had long necklaces–I don't know what else to call those chains with a Virgin hanging down over the windshield in front of the driver. A bus pulled up that was heading out to Arturo´s *colonia*, his sub-division. This bus like all the rest had a name. I boarded *Coraje*, Courage, its name painted in large letters so the driver had to look around it to see ahead.

A boy, about as big as the one this morning, jumped out the bus front door and watched as I finished climbing its four steps, about three feet up, into the bus. I dropped in four pesos and pushed towards the back with the other standing passengers. The boy banged three times on the side of the bus to let the driver know we all were either in or out and then jumped aboard as the driver jammed the bus into gear and we lurched forward.

It was packed, no place to sit. All seats were long taken at this time, the end of rush hour. I hunted for a corner to squeeze into, to hold me steady as we hit bumps and holes and the famous *topes*, mole hills, in Spanish. Mexican drivers know these foot-tall speed bumps that every community makes across the road to slow traffic in front of their houses; gringos learn quickly as they fly over the first time or two, or they buy a new suspension for their car.

It was hot. The windows had been opened but bodies trapped the air. I was lucky. My head was above most of the others, shorter people with Indian ancestors who did the hard work of this city and did not ride around in a Mercedes or even in old sedans.

We crossed the riverbed, passed by the new Walmart, MacDonalds and Chickylandia. That was Colonel Saunders playland in front of his red and white drive through. Then picking up speed we went by the turnoff to the airport and finally stopped at Arturo's new colonia, one of the developments the government was encouraging Mexico's middle class to buy into. This tract home suburb had a straight paved street lined with small concrete block houses, two stories, two bedrooms, comfortable enough, and a driveway in front, next to a small green ten-foot square lawn. Not walled in like in the real city. And a home loan, something not available a couple years ago, even though it cost twenty per cent a year.

Arturo was buying one of these for his family. He lived with only his wife and daughter. His parents and uncles and cousins were up in the mountains, wishing he had not left home after finishing his studies. But it was better than heading to el Norte, they thought. You took a job where you could, even if it meant a new un-Mexican way to live.

And living a ten hour drive away from your mother, even if you were in your 40's, was as un-Mexican as you could get.

I knocked on his door.

Arturo and his wife Carmen welcomed me. I entered and passed her small altar to the Virgin next to the door. I started to cross myself but, even after years here, was afraid I would screw it up–they do some kind of double pass with crosses everywhere starting at the lips, I think. No one puts this in the guidebooks for gringos–so I just nodded towards the altar and walked in.

I met Arturo ten years ago when I first came here for visits. His wife started me out in Spanish classes at the language school. Then I met her family. Arturo discovered I had studied hydrology, that is water stuff, like rivers and lakes, way back when I was young. I still could talk water planning and even read some of the journals on the internet. I had worked a long time writing environmental impacts so I knew my stuff.

After college, I started in water management but then made the big kiss-off compromise and moved to coal impacts, just to make enough for a family to live. Now that part of my life was over and Arturo and I dreamed and sometimes schemed about clean drinking water, year round, for the whole state down here in Mexico. Now the city only turned on the water mains every Tuesday and sometimes on Sundays in most of the *colonias* and barrios. Everyone tried to fill a big tank up on their roof when the water was on, but sometimes the tanks ran dry. Water here was not like in the States. You always knew how much you had in your tank. And you couldn't drink the city water anyway—everyone knew that.

Arturo offered me a beer. He was watching the news on the TV. Carmen went upstairs. She knew what had happened and left this to me and Arturo.

"You are famous." Arturo was speaking English now. He did that when something was important. He knew I got lost if the Spanish was too difficult.

"They are showing a picture of you with the boy on the evening news."

"Oh, no." I looked at the image on the screen.

"I think it is not too bad. Everyone wants to forget the old Governor. This shall pass soon. He ran away to California with our money and I do not think he has too many more problems like the Colonel to clean up. But, then, I don't know for certain."

"Is it safe for me?"

"Everyone wants to forget, and you should also. The boy has a rich widow mother. She and the child will live well somewhere like Spain. She has more than enough money to afford therapists to make the boy into a happy, well adjusted man. You must remember these are not real people. The rich are not real people."

I told him about the money and the man in the Santo Domingo Church. Arturo said they were helping my memory fade away. That was OK.

"Nothing is a crime here if the government does it. A political death makes the papers and the photos are everywhere for a day. Newspaper pictures hang on the street corners showing the messy results of political in-fighting. They are not martyrs for us normal people to rally around. We fight back, maybe quietly, but only when the politicians attack us, steal from us, not when they fight each other."

He held up the photo of me that was on TV. It was from the *sección roja* of the evening news. There I was, staring dumbly ahead, holding the boy. Bright red ink on the newsprint showed the spots on our clothes and the boy's blood-smeared face. The fancy Mercedes was rammed into the wall behind us.

"Who could have taken that?" I asked

"Maybe the press knew it was going to happen. Maybe it was luck. Who knows? Like I told you, he was evil and we have a new Governor. Let us not dwell on the past."

"The drug gangs did this?"

"No, they are in the north. If they did this you would be dead. They do not leave witnesses. I am sorry to say that, Roberto, but it is true. This was normal politics, cleaning up after an election."

"Great." I was thinking that our US politics are messy, but the politicians just stab each other in the back.

"You have your politics up north. You pay more and steal more. And you murder more people in the streets every day than we do in a year. At least here in Oaxaca."

"Now eat some *cena*–dinner–with us and have another beer and I will drive you home. I don't think this will affect you very much. You live quietly and you are a gringo. You have family in el Norte and no one here knows who your family might be, maybe a senator or some important man.

It is hard for us to figure you out in the US. You keep your families secret."

He was right. I was quiet. No one really knew about me. I spent my days going to restaurants. I read mysteries and geology and history books from the American Library. I studied Spanish. That was it. Exactly what a retired 65 year old ex-manager might do in Mexico if he got eased out of his job when he was fifty three, did his cancer early, recovered from it by spending all the savings that were left after the market ate his 401K. And his wife took off to find herself with her Wiccan friends. And their daughter joined the Rainforest Action people and cut off contact. Quiet is the right word for me. Maybe even shell shocked.

"And don't write about the shooting anywhere," Arturo added. "Stick to your restaurants and cooking school articles. Maybe something about the rains coming late."

I wrote articles for the expats and tourists in a local freebie throwaway. I wasn't thinking about writing anything about my morning.

That was it. Carmen came down stairs. We ate. Talked about how things were changing slowly. How it was getting better for many. Worse for many, too. And how his daughter was practicing Mexican dances, as we ate, at the churchyard down the street. And about how important water was in the world, Arturo's favorite subject.

It was just another normal day in Oaxaca.

Rabbit

Arturo was right. Not much happened.

The news photo of me with the boy got picked up by some papers in the States and they mixed it up with the war on drugs. I didn't complain. I figured complaining would make things worse, more complicated and prolong the assassination story. I wanted everything to die down.

I stayed away from the expat hangouts. They had little to do but recycle the latest happenings of their fellow gringos—who was sick, who was hooking up, and who finally gave up and headed back. And, now for the first time, who got caught in a shootout.

A week went by.

The leaders of the teachers strike made a deal with the new Governor. Most of the Federales left in their big black airplane. You could cross town without seeing lines of cops and marches of teachers.

I don't know exactly what they agreed on but everyone was sure big payoffs were involved. Not to the teachers, but to their leaders. Like normal. The teachers went home and the stolen government port-a-potties were recovered from the striker's makeshift campground in front of the municipal office buildings. The port-a-pottie story made the papers. The payoffs did not.

It was slow time. The yearly Oaxaca dance festival finished two weeks before; so most tourists had gone home. The streets looked busy, but it was only local craftspeople, running back and forth, trying to hawk their weavings or paintings or carvings to the few still left on vacation. During this time of year nothing but cheap tour groups showed up, booked into smaller hotels. Waiters and hotel maids took advantage of the slow season and went home to visit family in the villages. The remaining staff stood staring out at the street from their empty restaurants and hotels.

Señora Concepción finally saw my news photo and realized I was the gringo who grabbed the boy. Now she triple blessed me every time I walked by. Arturo called every couple days and asked how I was. He was sure all the fuss was over.

I sat in the lawn chair on my balcony sipping an iced tea in the shade of a large umbrella that I bought in a weak moment last year from the Walmart on the other side of the city. I usually tried to buy in the Oaxacan mercado, but sometimes slipped up and got things like this. The umbrella was a sensible brown. Not Mexican in any way. A Mexican one would have five colors so bright they hurt your eyes.

My geraniums on the other hand were very Mexican, not the feeble-stemmed varieties I had known in the States. They were fat, bunchy plants covered with lipstick red flowers sprawling from clay pots all around the balcony. It was beautiful up here, and comfortable, like my life in Mexico.

I looked down from my balcony watching one of the tours as it headed out from a hotel up the street. The guide waved the group's banner proclaiming "Fearless Adventures," all the while walking backwards and calling out the evening agenda to a few front-of-the-crowd listeners. The rest chatted and a few looked up at me. I watched the group pass and then a couple stragglers followed, older tired adventurers, looking pretty docile in the late afternoon sun. The stragglers carried beer cans from the hotel and dragged behind the main group complaining about yet another church that they were heading to see.

I never had been on a tour here. In fact, I didn't join anything. I was a real straggler in life. For the past week, though, I had been more than that–I had been a monk. Well, a monk with a nice balcony and lots of iced tea. I finished five mysteries and was pretty bored with the Byzantine Empire. I picked up its history from the American library down the street a couple weeks back and never had found time or interest to open it until all this started.

Before the murder, I thought I would like the solitary life, but this was too much. I was even ready to go spend a whole expat evening with Carlos and Lark.

I did not answer email. I did not return the phone messages that Señora Conception kept reminding me about. The press could not get past the front door and the Señora. I did not go out. But I watched the street. All seemed clear. I never saw anyone in a suit hanging around. No big cars. Nothing. It was time to go out.

I was getting hungry too. Tonight would be my breakout. I would get away from my room and eat something real, not the canned tuna and soups that I had been living off during my isolation.

I heard a soft knock on the door.

"Señor Roberto ¿*Está?*"

My landlady. I knew I had paid the rent. She likes us gringos who pay on time, something the Mexican tenants sometimes forget. Or maybe have trouble affording.

She did not come to my room often. I opened the door.

"*Buenas tardes*", I spoke in my limited Spanish. She spoke almost no English so we normally had fairly simple conversations about food and God. She was insistent upon the latter. I usually listened, nodded and thanked her when she ended up sending God´s blessings my way.

"*Perdón.* I am sorry to bother you. Were you resting?"

"No, no," I lied. "Please come in. Would you like something to drink? Please sit down."

I had mastered the rules of courtesy, so important here. You cannot just drop by quickly and you cannot ask why a visitor shows up, especially an older woman.

"Would you like something to drink?" I repeated. You have to offer food and drink, even if you know your visitor just ate.

She smiled and shook her head. Everyone knew I had that horrible gringo drink, iced tea, so no one ever wanted anything wet in this apartment.

"Then you must have a cookie, right from the bakery this morning." I had bought them as a gift for Arturo's family for when I would go back to visit. But we could finish these and then get more.

"Thank you, gracias." She never turned down a cookie. I believed it was the basis of our relationship. That and God. I never turned down a cookie or a blessing.

"Señor Roberto, I have a question, please." She paused for a moment. "You know Maria?"

Everyone knew Maria. She had been with the Señora for years, cooking and cleaning, from a village in the mountains that she visited two weeks every year. Sometimes a cousin or niece would visit Oaxaca for a day and stay in Maria's small room on the roof while Maria asked if anyone needed a maid or a driver or someone to clean in a restaurant. Then the visitor usually returned home or maybe headed up to el Norte.

About Maria, I should explain that everyone who had even a little money had a maid here in Oaxaca, especially the families of the older generation. Maids kept the hot water heaters running, bought the chickens, cooked everything, did the laundry, swept the patios, and helped the ladies of the house keep their altars.

"Maria needs to talk with you."

"Me?"

"Yes, she knows what you did for the boy and how you saved him. I know you do not want to talk of this but the priest told us to ask you. Can you talk with her?"

The priest was always the Señora's trump card. She was the one who told the priest what to say; then she repeated his words to stamp her ideas. I was not sure what was going to happen. Maria never asked anything. She always was just there. But you could never turn down a request from the Señora. I nodded yes.

Maria walked in quietly. She had been waiting outside the door.

I was a bit stunned that this happened so quickly. I could only think to ask, "A cookie for you, Maria?" I knew there was no use in offering her the famous, vile iced tea.

She took one and sat down.

"Señor Roberto, a problem has arisen." The Señora talked. Maria sat silently beside her.

"It is about Maria's niece Lupe. She chose not come to Oaxaca to work. She went to el Norte. She went two years ago. We heard from her at first. She wrote letters every month. She worked as a maid in Los Angeles for a famous rich doctor. Something happened. She has not written since Navidad, since eight months ago."

I realized that something had just quietly happened in my life too. I was no longer the old gordo gringo who read too much for his eyes according to the Señora. I was not just a long term tourist. I had joined Oaxaca in the Señora's eyes. She was asking my help.

This was a big deal. Her opinion was important. She was an institution in the *parroquia*, the neighborhood Catholic

45

Church that had a truly Mexican name: Sangre de Christo. She ruled the congregation, dominating the rituals and customs. She had put down several rebellions of younger women and once even of a young priest who wanted to make changes.

Most importantly, she was the person to see if you had a problem. Neighbors came to the Señora when they were sick and could not pay, or when there were problems with the daughter-in-law, or the electricity had been cut off, or it was time for a new dress for the life-size Virgin Mary that stood next to the altar in Sangre de Christo.

It looked like I had just become part of her network. I didn't know what else to call it. Not quite family, a web of people with obligations to the Señora. A network of connections to minor government officials, priests, curandera healers, merchants and sons of friends that worked in Mexico City, who fixed problems, sometimes with a small "gift" to an official or maybe a phone call to someone who had been helped before.

I am not sure exactly how, but now I was obligated to the Señora, at the least for her prayers and blessings and the three years of living next to her and her family. If I wanted to stay here and keep my standing as one of the acceptable gringos, I had to help.

My free touristy expat life had ended. Maybe it ended when I saw the shooting. Anyway it was over. I had responsibilities.

I talked with Maria, actually more with the Señora, speaking for Maria. I learned little about the doctor in LA except he had airplanes and big cars and all the other tools of the rich. I got his name, Bernard Marsden, and the fact that he lived in the rich part of Los Angeles with swimming pools and hills. And finally that he was a doctor of babies and children, which made him wonderful in the Señora's eyes. I could tell she thought the problem was with Lupe.

I knew from my mystery novels that I should speak alone with Maria. She probably knew a secret or two about Lupe that I could wring out of her, except I was not a detective. I was not sure exactly what I was these days. I said that I would look into it. Like one of the Godfather characters before he offed someone. Or at least beat them up. I planned to check and see if this guy existed on the web and maybe try to call. That sounded like a reasonable level of investigation. I was retired, after all.

The Señora was happy. Maria was crying like in a *telenovela*–a Mexican soap opera. A major part of the Mexican TV schedule was filled with these shows. Now I was seeing a live and in person show in my room.

Deep down, I wondered if I had gotten in over my head, especially while trying to lay low after my assassination problem. This Lupe thing looked small, unrelated and manageable. Best of all, I did not think it would affect me in my daily routine of espresso, walks, naps, books and Mexican food. And it might get me invited more often to the Señora's table for Maria's cooking.

I hugged Maria and the Señora and then saw her son Jorge coming back from work for his afternoon meal. I waved. He looked confused seeing the two women up the stairs in front of my room. They never came up here together. Maria came up and cleaned; the Señora came for the rent. In the courtyard, the grandchildren ran to their *papi*. He hugged them and walked into the dining room in the back of the courtyard where his wife was wondering about the meal that Maria had left bubbling on the stove.

I headed out the door. Still time for my late comida in one of the good restaurants. I was going to get out for some real food today, no matter what. A week holed up was enough.

It was hot. Not stifling, but hot enough to make me take it easy until the sun went down–no walking until then. I needed a taxi. Of course, the traffic was all jammed because of another blockade, this time some pueblo wanting to get their water supply repaired. Cars were sitting still. Everyone was honking. It gave drivers something to do.

I walked to my local cab stand and squeezed into the front seat of the only cab. I was too big for the backseat. My friend Efraím was driving. He drove everyday from seven in the morning to four in the afternoon, sharing the cab with his brother who did the night shift. They lived near Oaxaca in one of the pueblitos, the little villages down on the other side of the river. Efraím and his wife Lucia and his brother and his brother's wife and, every once and a while, a couple others who circulated in and out from his village four or five hours away. He was one of my Mexican friends that I met on weekends after he got off work, and we would go out and eat. And talk.

"*Hola*, Efraím. *¿Qué pasa?*"

"*Nada*, Señor Salvador. Next time save me when the ex-Governor comes around."

"I did not save anyone. I think someone fixed that picture with a computer program, el FotoShop. It wasn't me."

"*A dondé, mi amigo*? Where are we going?"

"Mi favorito, Dos Tíos Restaurante." I was starting to salivate making it hard to talk.

"Your favorite changes every week. Good you are not married. It would not last past a menu change down the street."

I did not pay attention. "I am hungry. I have not had much since the assassination."

"So you did do it!"

"No, it was a mistake. Some bad photo angle."

"*Bién*. Let's get out of here."

Efraím knew the back streets and we turned sharply and headed down a cobblestone alley. It ended at the dried-out riverbed. We drove along a twisting road running by the river bank—one of the few roads that did not point straight like a compass in this right-angle, gridded Mexican city. Then after about a mile he cut back to the main road and drove past a couple night clubs that were dead, waiting for the night. A block later Efraím stopped. The restaurant entrance was hardly marked. Only a small sign stood by the street, but everyone knew it. Mole sauces from the seven regions lured Oaxacans here: mole negro, mole colorado, mole verde, mole mixto, mole con Tasajo. I forget the rest. I was going to try them all tonight. My week of canned tuna with catsup while I was holed up had made me a little crazy. I was going to eat all seven.

The upper middle class went to Los Tíos. They knew their food. It was not a tourist place. Lots of suits and ties were the norm, mixed in with women: older women, mothers and aunts, in shawls, and younger wives in heels and dresses from Mexico City. And, of course, kids. The requisite restaurant playground was just out the back door in a small garden. Handmade sheet metal slides and swings, sharp edges everywhere, sat on a patch of concrete to catch any kiddies who fell. Children learned quickly about dangers here, like expats. Children learned faster, though. Even running around with fireworks in their small fists and riding on the handlebars of their parents' motorcycles, they seemed to do just fine. Of course, the press did not report accidents to children unless they were fatal, so, really, it was hard to say.

I walked in and the restaurant *dueño* greeted me. He was used to my solo eating adventures and motioned to a table in the back near the kitchen.

I walked through the thinned out crowd. It was almost 4 PM, getting late for the big afternoon lunch meal in Oaxaca. Two large family gatherings, no one else, were finishing family fiestas. Kids were out back yelling.

Then I saw the man. The man in the suit from Santo Domingo. The one who left the money. And he saw me. I looked down at my feet and headed quickly to my table. Leaving the restaurant seemed worse than staying. I felt a little dizzy.

And even worse, my appetite died.

I decided not to drink anything and asked for a plate of the antojitos Oaxaqueños-the specialty appetizers. They might revive me. I munched my way through some of the cheese and sausage chunks but had to order a beer to wash down the *chapulines*–the crunchy grasshoppers covered in chilies, kind of a high protein mini-chip. I wanted something plain in my dazed state so I ordered a grilled rabbit. I needed meat to strengthen me because it was obvious that the suit man was looking hard at me and something was going to happen.

Finally, his family gathering started breaking up. Several hugs and back pats later the man walked towards me. He waived back at the family smiling as they moved toward the door.

"Hello my friend, I see we have the same tastes in restaurants."

"Well, not in clothes." It blurted out before I had time to think.

"But you are from the north and have not learned the pride that we have here in Mexico. Comfort is not the only thing in life, is it? May I sit down?"

"Yes, would you like something to drink?" When you don't know what to do, be courteous. My mother taught me that when I was little. She could have been Mexican.

"Not now, I must leave with the family, but I wanted to thank you again. Nothing more appeared in the paper. You did well to avoid the press. I wish I could do so well with them."

I waited. Maybe out of fear. Maybe because this was all so strange to me.

"I have been planning on coming to see you. About something else. I would like to talk with you."

"What would you want to talk to a tourist about, anyway?" This was not going in a good direction.

"I understand you are an expert on many things. You were quite famous in some circles. I had to read your reports on coal mines when I was in college several years ago. We have mines here you know. You must come to see me and we can talk about the wonderful land here in Oaxaca."

He knew about me.

"But that was years ago," I started explaining. "And that was my company, not me." I thought I had left those days behind, the days when I was writing environmental reports. My daughter said I sold out. But then it paid for her fancy college degrees. Now she sat in front of bulldozers and nursed sick seagulls. And sometimes sent me eco-news clippings. That was all I got from her.

"Let us talk. I insist." He handed me a business card. Señor Dr. Licenciado Alfonzo Ruiz, Director of a long involved name, a government agency in Oaxaca. I looked up at him as he reached out again to shake my hand.

"You must not think so badly of us. We are a good people trying to live through hard times. For instance, the Colonel's family was meeting here and strengthening their ties today. We all should do that when we have a loss in the family."

"My condolences." The boy was not with the family. This really confused me now. I thought back to Arturo's advice. "This will go away," he told me. He forgot that nothing ever goes away. He forgot that men like the Colonel in the Mercedes are not alone. They have their connections and families, like the Señora, but at a different level. The connections go on. Like a hydra-head octopus, injured, with one leg cut off, limping and angry.

Señor Ruiz walked out the door and did not look back. This required more beer. Quick. And some mezcal. A couple.

Donuts

"Damn, I'm hurting."

Head, muscles, stomach. It was the cheap Chilean wine on top of the beer and mezcal. I got carried away last night when I needed to forget how confusing things were at the restaurant, so I zoned out, opened a bottle of wine and watched a movie on cable. Lots of horses, sombreros and a couple faked fistfights. I nodded off late.

The morning noise sounded louder than normal. Normal was pretty loud. But today a jackhammer out in the street banged away in addition to daily chorus of honking and yelling. I needed a jolt of espresso to clear my head and help turn down the volume in my brain.

I was late for my morning caffeine. Yesterday I had planned on making a triumphant return to the expat world early this morning after my week of self-imposed exile. But it would be not so triumphant after last night's excess. I took a long shower. I would hear about that from the Señora. The water tank on the roof was probably half gone when I finished and the gas–I probably drained the propane tank.

Right on cue, the propane man drove by. "Gaz de Oaxaca" blared out the loudspeaker on his small truck.

I was bearing the noise now, barely. Chains dangled from the gas truck's rear axle ringing like bells as they clanged on the cobblestones. The water man came by yelling, *"Agua. Gua. Gua."* He sputtered past on his new motorized three-wheeler. Funny, how I never listened to this cacophony much before. It took a good hangover to open my ears to Oaxaca. Church bells started ringing. Then the primary school classes added a loudspeaker blasting some inept voice singing a marching song.

The noise actually helped. It hurt but kept me from remembering much about the night before in the restaurant. I knew I would have to figure out what to do soon, but for now, I just wanted my espresso and maybe a couple of the big *donas*–donuts–which had become part of the culinary life in Mexico, along with the tamales and tortillas and fried grasshoppers.

I was heading down the steps when I heard a new voice, "Mister Evans. Oh, Mister Evans."

I tried to get back in the room but had made too much eye contact with the woman standing at the bottom of the steps. Fuzzy hair, big hat, big glasses, shortish skirt, bunchy blouse and skimpy sandals. Behind her a man about the same age, mid 50s, another big hat, lots of white sunscreen, Hawaiian shirt, shorts and hiking boots. No camera.

55

"Mister Evans," the woman continued, "oh, we are so lucky to catch you. The Señora told us about you and how you help people. How you helped the boy in the shooting. We are here to do the same. Help, that is"

I was thinking that they could help themselves to the assassins, any time, but then my mother's and the Señora`s courtesy lessons kicked in.

"Wonderful, wonderful, I know that the Oaxacans are glad you are here."

"Yes, we are your new temporary neighbors in the apartment on the other side and are volunteers looking for a place to help. We want to share our good luck in the United States with the world."

I have to admit that volunteers are a lot better than the evangelists with their skinny ties, black suits and nametags, prowling the streets for converts and handing out Spanish tracts with kodachrome God pictures. Evangelists don't want us expats; we scare them. We show where western civilization can lead.

"My name is Rob and this is Clara. We are retired." The man spoke up.

I came down and shook their hands looking for a quick getaway out the open door to the street.

"I was an engineer and can do construction. Clara was a nurse and would love to teach."

Everybody wanted to teach or show the local people what to do. No one wanted to dig holes or chip rocks, like the men working in the street today, next to the jackhammer, destroying their hearing. I looked out the doorway and could see a dozen men in their white traditional village pants and shirts. The workers' feet stuck out of handmade sandals and I wondered how many toes they would have left when they reached forty.

They had five picks, five shovels and a hole about six feet by six feet in the middle of the road. Men inside the hole, only visible as straw hats poking up, threw dirt out in shovelfuls every ten seconds or so. Their jackhammer burst out every few seconds. It was near the truck, away from the digging. The jackhammer guy was a big shot in jeans, waiting for men with wheelbarrows to bring him big chunks of pavement. Then he grabbed the jackhammer, looked important, and broke everything into small chunks. Other guys, the lowest on the totem pole, I think, picked up little chunks and tossed them into an old dump truck. That was not the way we dug street holes in the States, but it worked and lots of people had jobs. With room left over for some volunteers.

"The Señora thought you must know places that needed us," Clara interrupted the noise yelling.

I wanted to suggest helping the guys on the street and, maybe, buying them steel toed boots, too. But again that courtesy got me. "You know the best place to ask is at the American Library near the park. Anyone who looks like an expat–they will know where it is."

Expats go there to borrow DVDs to watch after they get bored volunteering. I didn't say that though.

"Oh, thank you, Mister Evans. The Señora was right."

"Call me Roberto, and now I am sorry but I have an appointment and need to go."

I walked at a fast clip and got out the door before they could answer.

Five minutes later I was in La Avenida and, of course, Carlos was sitting at a table. I was hoping some of the others would be inside too. None were. Most people leave you alone if you looked annoyed or hung over. Carlos never noticed. He just started talking.

I got my espresso and Carlos came to the counter next to me.

"We all thought you went the way of the Colonel, when you disappeared." He laughed his horsey, all-American laugh.

"I was not involved. Sorry, I have an appointment, Carlos. Got to run."

I made my second escape of the morning, walked quickly into the park and chugged the espresso. Then I headed for my appointment–it was with a donut at the bakery, a block away. Inside you picked up a tray and metal tongs and grabbed what you wanted from the long displays of pastries, cookies and loaves of bread stacked around the interior walls. I plopped three big donuts on the tray, one with sugar, one covered in chocolate and one plain. The sugar should clear things out in my head. The sugar and another espresso, that is. I paid and went to the patio of the next door hotel and finished off my three round guys, dunking them into my second espresso, not as good as La Avenida, but without any expats to slow me down.

I took a mental health day after the donuts, just walking around my favorite colonia, the Reforma, up north of the Centro, where a lot of the middle class Mexicans lived. I figured that not thinking about what was happening would give my brain time to recover a little. What do they call it when you figure things out when you don't think, subconscious thinking? Well I was doing it—not a conscious thought stirring upstairs in the worrying part of my brain, the part that I knew way too well.

I walked north at a good pace. Here, the walls were not so high, but the houses were still hidden. Every other corner had a prep or preschool; no one with money sent their kids to public schools around here. In private schools, teachers couldn't strike all the time.

I passed the colonia's restaurants and small shops on its two main streets: a produce shop with a fifteen-foot wide stucco avocado on the roof, a piñata stand with paper maché Disney characters hanging like they had just been found very guilty, and enough hair and nail shops for every woman to get done up simultaneously, just like in the States. For men there was a barber shop. Five barbers clipped away in front of a wall-long mirror—a real barber shop, the kind I grew up with. A red and white pole out front that reminded you they drew blood if not careful. On the shelves sharp things, scissors and straight razors, poked up from jars of blue disinfectant. I saw no electric clippers. Women's hair places had new little battery ones; men down here wanted their faces near sharp-edged steel, maybe to wake them up in the morning. A little fear is good for that.

My old Baltimore barber shop was like that. And it had hunting and car magazines and pinup ones, too, just like here. They shaved the back of my neck with a straight razor when I was sixteen and old enough, scraping close so alcohol burned when they rubbed it on. Then it ended. I grew long hair, went to college and left Baltimore and its barber shops for good.

Now I favored electric clippers–less blood; so I usually went to the unisex shop across the street where you saw younger Mexicanos, middle class ones, not the barber shop's old, grizzled faces that must have been hell for barbers to shave with a straight razor. But I liked looking in the window and remembering the old days. That is one reason I am here, I am sure.

I walked a couple hours, avoiding the Los Tíos Restaurant on the edge of the Colonia where I saw Ruiz and his family. I did not want another chance encounter like the day before. Or maybe worse, a planned one.

I ended my walk with a meal. That was my normal walk plan. This time at the Che Restaurant where they brought raw chunks of meat out for your selection. Just like in Argentina–that's what they told me. I picked a steak, about two pounds and dripping blood when they held it up. They cooked it, sort of. It seemed dead so I ate it—chewy–but the mezcal helped tenderize everything, including me.

Comida is the best time of the day in Mexico. It is the center of everything. Only I was alone and that broke the number one comida rule. But I was on good terms with the steak so it was ok.

I was ready for whatever might come after eating that thing, but decided to go home and take a nap. It was siesta time.

I rested an hour or so and then waking up, figured I should do something for Lupe. The Señora had a two day cycle for her requests so I knew she would check with me tomorrow if I didn't say anything tonight. I wanted to give her some news. I got out my laptop and searched for the doctor. There he was. Lots of degrees—a professor at UCLA Med School. Getting his home address was harder. It was easy to discover that he was 53, owned a house worth a couple million, was not a Facebook friend to anyone, had a wife and two others at his house, but all the web sites wanted $3.99 a month for a year to let me know his address and phone number. I tried the Med School and nailed him. 499 Sierra Mar Lane, Beverly Hills. Looked it up in the satellite photos on Google: a big pool and a little one too, and a wrap-around drive. Big house. Must take a lot of cleaning by Lupe. I did a reverse phone lookup from the address and got the number. I took out my headset and made a call through the internet. It sounded underwater but it was cheap.

"Hello, is this Dr. Marsden's residence?"

A woman speaking with a Spanish accent answered yes.

"Is Lupe there? I am calling for her family from Mexico."

"I am having trouble understanding you. Did you say Lupe? She left about a month ago. Said she was going to live with her family in Merced. Now who did you say you were?"

"I am a friend of the family who speaks English. Lupe's aunt works where I live and asked me to see what happened to her."

"I have an address and number for her. I will go look for it. Can you wait a minute?"

It took a couple minutes. I copied down the information and thanked the woman. She never did say who she was. She sounded Mexican and was most helpful. *Muy amable* is what they would say down here. Everyone is willing to help here. They offer so many helping hands that doing something takes twice as long. Everyone chips in. I was glad to see that *muy amable* got transplanted to LA, a place I usually think of as zero *amable*.

I looked up the satellite photo for the Merced address. Looked like the wrong side of the tracks. No sidewalks. Lots of little frame houses. A big difference from Beverly Hills.

That was easy. Maybe I was a detective after all. At least for old Mexicans who don't know about the web yet.

Time for a reward. I grabbed an iced tea and headed out for the easy chair on the balcony.

———

"Well that is fine, but why did you not call Lupe?"

I saw the Señora on my way out after my siesta. I thought I had done a pretty good job getting the address. She wanted more than information. She wanted Lupe.

"I will do that tomorrow." I started to add God willing, but realized that God willing or not, the Señora expected me to make the call. No getting out of this one.

"Please! I will tell Maria. You will find Lupe, I am sure. God bless you."

No hugs this time. I was working for the Señora now.

I headed out on the street again, this time to the American Library, the hangout for the expats. Bridge club on Thursdays, monthly history lectures, yoga classes, two book clubs and a garden tour every spring. Mostly it was a place where people went to speak their English and live out a suburban backyard American life for an hour or two.

The building had about ten rooms filled with books and cataloged by retired expat librarians who couldn't keep their hands out of the old business.

I walked into its courtyard filled with folding tables and plastic lawn chairs. About a dozen people sat in small groups talking and drinking. Francesca, she used to be Frances back in New York, ran the checkout desk. Rules on the desk warned that you could only have four books at a time, but all the volunteers let you do what you wanted, as long as they knew you.

"Hi, Francesca."

"Oh Roberto, you are back."

I decided right then to let everyone think I had gone away for the week.

"We were getting worried, what with the problems and all that." She was smiling like she just found an old high school friend. One that she thought had croaked.

Some people did not like to get too specific about the politics and crimes down here. They call them problems and that's that. But would rant for hours about the mess the Republicans had gotten us into in the States. Others loved to go on about the crooked politicians in Mexico, but only to other Americans.

Lance, one of the regulars, walked up. "Hey, they let you out?"

Gringo men joke about everything: getting locked up, wife leaving you, getting tortured. Mexican men kept quiet.

"Someone bake you a cake with a key inside?"

Not funny, not even a joke–just a soft poke in my ribs done with words.

"I just thought it better to go away for a while. But I am back and wanted say hi and maybe pick up a new book."

Carlos came over. "It was a Colonel, right?"

I didn't have to talk any more that night. Lance answered for me. "Yes, the Colonel got it. He was from an important family up on the hill."

Everyone knew that the politicians and the rich lived up the hill about two miles from the city. The army camped nearby as well; I thought to protect them. This was where the rich Type Two expat Texans kept their community too. Not many of them came down to the library with its Type Ones and books. I don't think they were readers, more likely satellite TV people, not noticing they were in Mexico, watching all the US shows.

Francesca waited her chance. "Yes, he was in internal affairs. They say he ran the vigilante groups for the ex-Governor. The ones that kidnapped the teachers and shot that American reporter a couple years back."

Everyone stopped for a moment remembering the big street takeovers three years ago when a revolution almost happened here after the teachers strike got ugly. Government men rode around in pickups firing guns, usually over the strikers' heads but one time they hit a reporter from the States. Who knows how many Mexicans got hit. Newspapers go crazy when one of their own gets it. US papers had barely reported anything before he got shot, not even when a hundred thousand protesters jammed the highway to the city or when the police ran for their lives and left the city, running from the teachers union, which took over the city for a month.

Funny how a gringo murder brought things to a head and the State Department put Oaxaca on the bad list and the expats took off for high ground, some back to the States and some to other expat communities a bit north or even down in Guatemala.

"Well good riddance." Lance raised his glass of wine. "Good work, Roberto."

"Hey, I didn't have anything to do with…"

"Sure. And that was not you in the picture. And are you not our new city saint? They say the local women are hanging your picture in some of the churches now. Saving us. Are you sure you were not involved? Maybe you did a little work for the Governor?"

He knew he went too far with that poke. Expats lived on the surface of life down here. You did not dig too deep about anything–especially connections to any government, US or Mexican. Lance knew it was time to ease up.

"Come on Santo Roberto, Santo Gordo. We needed a patron saint for the expats. All of us are just glad you got back and don't have too many bruises. Have a glass of wine or maybe we could find you a glass of iced tea if you wanted it."

Iced tea was included in most of the stories about me.

The expats were one of my families. I like to think of them as distant relations. I was stuck with them. Everybody has someone they are stuck with. These were mine.

I sat down and Francesca changed the subject and started telling what happened at the party last Saturday when Lynn and John showed up. They usually only came in the winter.

Most of the group moved to Carlos' rooftop later for the normal evening gathering after the library closed at 8 PM. I went along and heard a lot of theories about the shooting as the evening and the wine progressed. Narcos are moving south to take over production Narcos are moving north to take over distribution. Teachers got even. Villagers got back at the State government. The CIA is moving in. But no one said anything about the ex-Governor silencing his man.

I was in even less agreement with Arturo after hearing the night's discussion. He had assured me that life would go back to how it was before, but he was wrong. Things were changing. I was different from the rest of the expats on the roof. I was becoming a saint.

The Maria and Lupe story was going around the city. I am sure Maria told the next door neighbor and she told her friends and the next thing–the whole town heard I was available for little miracles. I had become Santo Gordo, part of the Oaxacan pantheon, or even worse, some of them called me El Santo, like the famous Mexican film wrestler, a bit on the heavy side, who saved people when he wasn't in the ring. But I let everything slide over me that night. Denying anything only seemed to get more stories going.

I realized something else listening that night. The expats were scared. They knew that when the violence got bad, their easy life here was over. They would take off fast and let everything Mexican go to hell, like it had up around the US border. But everyone hoped poor old Oaxaca was worth so little that no narcos or worse would want to fight over it.

I walked home, hands in my pockets, a mezcal or two in me, thinking how great it was to not worry too much about crime in what was still a pretty safe city. Then I thought about the Colonel and my man in the suit, Señor Ruiz, and started worrying. I needed to go see him soon. Before he came to see me.

Wednesday

Tuna Fish Casserole

The next morning I decided to look official when I showed up at Senior Ruiz' office. I was not normally one of the regular tourist slouches–I wore khakis with a crease, at least for the first day I had them on. I got my shoes shined every week or two and even had my shirts done in the laundry that irons them, just no starch, especially when it was hot. I admit I was not a style horse like some of the Mexican businessmen. And I did button my shirt to the neck, no half-bared chest like the macho types you saw in fancy restaurants with their weekend girlfriends.

I grabbed a jacket, tweedy like a professor, to finish getting set. Good outfit for a retired manager during interrogation. I was going to an interrogation. A smiling one probably, but this was not going to be fun. I was certain of that.

I wanted to look civilized, Mexican style, when I showed up for my meeting so I went to the park and climbed into one of the shoeshine chairs. I pulled my feet up on the ancient metal foot stands in front. The shoeshine man folded his newspaper and squatted down on an impossibly short wooden stool–maybe six inches tall, in front of my feet. He pulled out his box of brushes and rags and worked over my old walking shoes for ten minutes. I read his newspaper, skimmed through the normal politics and barricades stuff and saw a couple bodies lying in the *Sección Roja*—just run-over ones, not shot dead ones.

When the shoeshine man finished and I looked down, the sun reflected off my toe tips until it hurt my eyes. I gave him a big tip–about a dollar fifty for the whole thing, shine and tip, and he was happy. I was too. Civilized, happy and ready.

I walked the three or four blocks to Ruiz' office and looked at his overdone, converted colonial palace across from the Oaxaca museum. Palace was the right word for this place with carved stone columns and statues and fountains. Over the doorway was the name, "The Office of the State of Oaxaca for the Development and the Preservation of Indigenous Lands, State Parks and the Environment," OSODPILSPE. A real government-type name, filling about 10 feet of recently carved stone. I walked in.

The receptionist had a skirt so tight and short it was ready to pop up over her waist. Her blouse was form-fitted and stretched tight over lots of her up-top form. Big shots went for receptionists who looked like they came straight off the line at Vegas. She sat down carefully and managed to hold everything in place.

"The Licenciado is expecting you, por favor."

Big shots also liked big titles like licenciado. Even little guys liked big titles. You took anything you could to get a leg up down here. For some, a title was all they had. So they hung on to it pretty hard. And plastered it everywhere. Just like the big shots.

I ended up waiting about an hour. Just so I knew who was in charge.

He came out all smiles and hand extended. I stood and he ushered me into an office big enough house several Oaxaca families. It had a view of the botanical garden and was filled with probably not faux Spanish colonial furniture. He motioned to a chair that looked like the ones the Spanish brought over in their wooden ships, maybe for use in the inquisition. It was all right angles, corners, and over the edge of painful. I sat forward. Senior Ruiz had his Aeron super black, probably costing a year's salary for the average worker. It was cranked up so he could look down at me.

"Thank you for coming to meet."

"My pleasure." Funny, how being courteous makes you fake pleasure.

We continued our courtesy dance for a couple more minutes. Then he started talking about Mexico. A different dance.

"How do you find it here this year in Oaxaca?"

More dancing. He led.

"Most beautiful, this is the best month with the rain every afternoon." No lie from me there.

"I see you are a resident now. How wonderful. I hope you have come to love the country as we do."

I gushed about Oaxaca. He gushed. We all loved it here.

"And you know so much about the landscape, the environment, working so long with the developers in your country. You in el Norte have truly learned to appreciate the beauty of the land."

And how to rip it up. I helped destroy a good chunk of West Virginia, slicing off mountaintops to get at coal a while back. I was still paying for that. My environmentalist daughter would not talk to me and my wife, I mean ex-wife, was out hugging trees to make up for my evil days. But my feelings did not seem like something to bring up just then with Señor Ruiz. I figured he knew all about what I did back then anyway.

"I understand you are an expert on mining and its effect on the environment?"

"That was a long time back. Now I only enjoy the beauty of the land. Actually, I did not do mining, I only wrote reports. I have not worked for some time." Not working was thanks to the company that sacked me when they could line up cheap college grads—I did not tell that to the Señor, either.

We went over what I knew and what I did not. I claimed nothing, he claimed way much too much and seemed to know everything about me.

"We, too, have been developing our own environmental reports, not just for our government, but for the World

Bank and for others that will be investing in the development of our Oaxaca. But we are not expert in how the Americans will read the report. We would appreciate you reading it and letting us know if you think we should make changes."

"But surely, you should contact a company in the States, one with contacts and current experience." I was trying to sound as formal in my Spanish as he was.

"You know el Norte. If we send a draft proposal, then it will be on the web the next day. You have a most leaky country, we do not. Our employees are faithful citizens."

He meant that they might get shot if they posted something on the web.

"We are just asking for a friendly reading before we send it to our partner in the United States, a reading by someone who understands us in Mexico and also understands thinking in the United States. Someone like you, Señor Evans.

So here it was. They wanted me to vet their plan. And find its holes so that they could patch them up before they presented it to their stateside partners. And critics.

"We thank you, Senior Evans. You may come to this office to read the report at any time."

"I do not do this sort of thing anymore."

"Señor Evans, we would appreciate your help. You are a foreign national here in Mexico and we know you would like to stay. And we can help make that easy. As we agreed a moment ago it is a beautiful here in the south."

This was it. The strangle hold. My residence visa was coming up for renewal in three months. It was supposed to be automatic, but automatic did not sound like the right word anymore. I was thinking that a final squeeze would be coming up soon from Ruiz to end our little wrestling match. I already knew who was going to win. It was not me.

"We would like to help you stay. Would you like to get dual citizenship? We could help, especially if you could show our government how much you want to provide assistance to our country. After all, this is not just a playground for Americans. Not a Disneyland with chilies and Mariachis. We are a proud country. We need to grow. We need to create jobs and develop the land."

I loved the way he could make it sound so reasonable. I bet jobs meant a couple bucks a day, maybe less, sweating in a big hole in the ground and development would mean something poisonous, like in West Virginia.

"And there is that affair with the police and the shooting. I am sure that we can help you explain. I am sure that you were only helping the boy."

I tried not to react. I thought the police investigation was over but, as I kept finding out, down here events tend to linger, especially dealing with the government, the powerful and the police. I was learning it over and over, no matter what Arturo had said. I was sure Ruiz could and would get me booted from Mexico if I said no. Our match was over.

I tried to appear thoughtful, looking down at his desk at the bound papers which he held lightly—obviously the draft report. I wanted to act like I had a choice, but only for my dwindling pride. The deal was done. I would sweeten the report for gringo ears and they would sweeten my time down here. Or at least extend it a little. I looked to see the title, "Caballero Gold Fields." Gold, not coal. They both come in lumps and it takes holes in the ground to find them. Sounds close enough. At least for Señor Licensiado Ruiz.

I told him that I would come back the next day and read the report. A reading desk and a computer were to be made available to me for writing notes in an empty office down the hall where I could work in peace. I didn't think I would have a whole lot of peace doing this. At least not in my head.

I walked home slowly. I was never proud of what I had done back in the States. But I had been good at it. Sometimes it pays to be a slouch; then you don't get asked for a second go.

I headed back for the apartment. Not quite time for comida. I passed the big hole in the street in front of the house and I saw men still down there. Others on the street were mixing cement with hoes and then hauling it in buckets over to the hole.

People knew how to work here in Mexico; but then they had no choice. It reminded me of the States before we became a nail gel, computer game country, back when we used to make real stuff. My father and uncles worked in the shipyards where they welded and did all the other things you do to steel. My father said I would never go there. He was right. Those guys do haul-butt, sweat-and-callous work; I did desk jockey, carpel tunnel, waist-popping work. They died young; I will die fat.

Something seemed right to me about seeing people actually making something, digging holes with shovels-not backhoes, nailing with hammers-not those fancy air guns and pouring cement from wheelbarrows-not big pumping trucks. Doing something besides doodling at meetings and looking at computer screens. Something that took a little sweat.

No caution tapes or plastic roadwork barricades were set up to stop people in the street and keep them away from the big construction hole in front of my place. After all, this was Mexico. So I walked up and looked in. Four men, about eight feet down, were pouring buckets of concrete into a wooden form. No hard hats, no eyewear, no gloves. OK, maybe this kind of work was something you could only get nostalgic about if you didn't ever do it. The men did not look up. I figured someone was watching them.

I crossed the street and headed to the door in the wall that led to my place. A woman was standing there looking straight at me.

"Señor Roberto, you must help us, save us from the volunteers."

This was not good. The woman started walking toward me. She was Mexican, maybe 40, dressed in a skirt and blouse, lipstick, big heels. How could anyone wear heels and move through these cobblestone streets? Of course all the middle class Mexican women did. She picked her way without a wobble.

"The Library said you sent the volunteers. I need your help. Everyone says you can help."

Damn that picture of me and the boy. There was no escape; she was blocking the way to my door. What were their names, Rob and Clara? What were those two doing anyway?

"Señor Rob is painting the hall at our day care center. He said he was an engineer and it needed painting."

Everything needed painting in Oaxaca, I thought. Paint here lasted about a month in the sun and dryness.

"He is scrapping off the old paint. He is working many hours every day."

"How wonderful," I said.

"Anyone can scrape off paint. I can scrape off paint. There are men in the street who would scrape off paint for a meal. A small meal. Why would an engineer do that? He should design a new building for us. We need one."

"But he likes to help," I offered meekly.

I was thinking about the crazy gringo Protestants that come here to work off their sins. Protestants have no confession like the Catholics so they have to find something else to do. Rob found paint scraping. How could I explain this to a good Catholic lady? She knew the priest would give fifty Hail Marys if she did something bad or maybe just thought something non-Catholic. She did not have to figure out her penances. There was a formula. But we Protestants had to be creative.

"Señora, Señora. Let us go inside and we can have something to drink and talk about this."

She seemed happy that she had met a civilized gringo for a change, one who wanted to sit inside where it was cool and maybe have a drink or a cookie before getting to the problem. Problems first is not the Mexican way. You sneak up on problems.

"My name is Señora Alfreda Velázquez. I am the Directora at the neighborhood preschool center in our colonia down by the river."

We sat in the courtyard. I brought down two glasses of iced tea from my apartment. Señora Velazquez tasted it and held it politely. The Mexican cookies were better received. I asked about her family and where she lived. We talked ten minutes, politely. Then she started.

Your amigos came to us last week and said that you sent them to help us."

So according to this Directora and probably everyone else, they were my friends and it was me who sent them to her. I sent them to the American Library, not to her, but, I suppose, I did start the chain reaction going. I would not quibble.

"They are most thoughtful people, not Catholics they told us, but here to help. We did not need help, but they were Americanos and you know how we have to be with them."

She had let me join her side.

"Señor Rob decided to paint and now he is asking us to buy paint and we do not have money. And Señora Clara wants to teach us to cook. She wants to give a class on something baked and we do not have an oven and it requires *atun*. In a can. And some special pasta from America."

Ah, the great American tuna fish and macaroni casserole. Those two volunteers were small town Midwest, an all-American type that the foodie revolution obviously skipped.

"She wants us to buy cans of *atun*. We can get fresh fish. Why does she want cans? They cost more. You know we do not charge the families and the state gives us no money. We only have the building. What can we do?"

"Did you try telling them no?" Obviously this idea had not crossed her mind. Telling a gringo no, that was hard to do here.

"I will talk to them." I said.

"Thank you Señor Roberto. I knew that you would help." She crossed herself a couple times and then left.

What would I tell those volunteers? Cool it? Enough scraping? Learn to cook, don't teach it? I would figure it out later. Now it was time for a drink–stronger than iced tea, I think–some time on the balcony, and a good night's sleep.

Huevos Rancheros

The next morning was clear. It was chilly in Oaxaca's mountain valley most every morning, even in the summer, but everyone here thinks that my chilly is their icy cold.

I looked out from my balcony and watched people heading to work, some wearing bulky sweaters, some with faces wrapped in scarves, a couple with parkas. Oaxacans marveled at us gringos who wore tee shirts and shorts when it was fifty degrees; I marveled at their suits, ties and sweaters worn in the afternoon when it got over ninety.

It was time to quit gawking and get dressed. Ruiz was waiting for me. My pants crease was gone and shirt wrinkled, but I would be OK. I was only going to read and write today and not see anyone.

I had thought about the report all night. Actually I thought about all the reports I had written in my life. One more would not get me any deeper into hell.

I stopped for breakfast: Espresso–it was OK, Huevos rancheros–wonderful. The waiter–*amable*. I was ready after that and walked straight to Ruiz' office.

His receptionist wore a different outfit, but just as much showed. I followed her, watched her swinging those hips to the rhythm of her steps, not for me, just out of habit. She led me to my room and handed me the fancy bound papers of the report.

It was done well. Someone had gone to a top notch school up in the States to write a report like this, tailored for the gringos. It had a Spanish and English version. I stuck with the English, what anyone up north would read.

Here is the project plan made simple: Dig a hole. A big hole. It will take years. Get out the gold ore. Protect the land everywhere while digging. (Or make people think you are.) Put aside clean-up money every year out of the profits. Then sometime around 2030 cover everything back up. Plant trees. Import some deer. Easy. No impact.

I saw opportunity right away. Someone would collect and administer the protection and restoration fund, holding money for twenty plus years and not spending much until the digging was over. Of course, he would do protection work, building dams and keeping the heavy metals out of the ground water, but that would be cheap compared to putting the dirt and rock back in the hole. If you dig twenty years, guess how long it takes to put everything back. Twenty years is a pretty good estimate if everyone stays motivated. But gold is a lot more motivating than hole filling.

In twenty years someone would be sitting on his pile of gold drained from the protection fund, living either in a fat suburb of Mexico City or in fancy Europe. Even if things went poorly and he upset the dinosaurs and assassins, he would be lying in a big marble mausoleum, the kind that only the super rich dead can afford, with at least a yacht, a couple sportscars and a who knows how many trophy girlfriends in his wake.

I figured Ruiz would be that guy. He would make a killing. Then pass on the empty hole to the poor *pendejo* who followed him. That guy would have to fill it from the empty bank account. He would go to jail; OK, probably not to jail in Mexico. But Ruiz, he would be in heaven, or close to it, after leaving a pile to the Church. It was one hell of a plan.

One problem: the plan forgot the poor. It would not fly, especially with the World Bank and the press. What about the people who lived where the mine would be dug? The report said nothing. I bet Ruiz was going to argue no one lived there. I planned to take a look at the satellite photos.

Enough for today. I had read it all. I told the receptionist I was coming back the next day to finish writing. She twisted to keep everything in place as she stood and then asked to see my notes. I didn't ask to see anything of hers. I didn't need to.

"The Licenciado has requested that you leave all your work here. I will hold on to your things for you."

I had to get out quick. It would have been way too easy to make some snappy, bad detective comeback that would get me into trouble. I headed out through the stone columns, past the angel statues and through the gate with the pointed crosses woven into the ornamental ironwork. No one was going to get into there and see the report without official permission. That was for sure.

I was feeling blank after my work, not feeling anything much after joining the official Ruiz team today. I thought I had left this kind of operation behind in the States.

Then I felt it–hunger, that is. But there was still time before comida would be ready in the restaurants. I was not like the tourists who started looking for a table at noon, asking for a light lunch. I did a 2 or 3 PM arrival, when the good cooks were in the kitchen and the real Mexican food was ready. Tourists wanted the afternoon for themselves after something quick, but Mexicans knew that the afternoon belonged to food and maybe a friend or some of the family.

I had an hour or so to kill. Might as well head back and call up Maria's missing niece Lupe in Merced. That would keep my mind off food. Time for another job by Santo Gordo.

I called the phone number in Merced that I got from the doctor´s house the day before.

"*Bueno*," a woman answered.

"Lupe, *por favor*?" I asked. The line was quiet for a few seconds

"*No hay Lupe aquí.*" She hung up.

Not there? That was quick. I called the doctor's number again, the one I called yesterday, the one where she gave me Lupe´s number, to check if I had it right. I got a different voice from yesterday. No accent this time. Clipped English today.

"I am sorry but the person speaking with you yesterday should not have given out the telephone number. She has been counseled about privacy issues. I understand your concern but we are sorry, we cannot help you." Bam.

Another call cut short. I was just trying to make sure the number was correct. Something was fishy.

I decided to call the Merced Lupe number again, but this time I would let Maria talk. If Lupe were there, then a friendly voice would be hard for her to resist. Then, my job would be done, mission accomplished.

Mission was the right word for doing this. I had been sent by Señora Concepción on one of her holy tasks. Not quite a full scale God-job like the priests did when they came to convert Mexico's Indians, but close. That was how everyone would look at it—Santa Gordo off on another quest.

Maria was washing clothes. She had her hands in a concrete wash tub filled with soapy water, a tub like the ones that used to be in my Baltimore basement, where the washing machine pumped out dirty water. But no washing machine was here, just Maria. Her concrete tub had a cement washboard and she rubbed the pilled-up white cloth, maybe a sheet or two, up and down against the washboard's wavy edge.

"Maria, please. Can you talk with Lupe?"

"I am washing now. The Señora needs her wash finished." The Señora controlled Maria's day. It was even stronger than that. Maria was part of the Señora, the chapped hands and bent over shoulders part. The part that washed and washed when the Señora said so.

"But the Señora would want you to help find Lupe."

Maria must have been waiting for an out because she answered quickly. "If the Señora desires me to do it."

We went up to my room and I telephoned Lupe in Merced again. The phone rang several times. I handed the headset to Maria.

Suddenly Maria called out, "Lupe, Lupe, Lupe, it is me. It is Maria. Lupe, Lupe, answer."

Then a response. I couldn't make out the little voice on the phone.

Maria turned to me. "It is Lupe." She smiled and started crying.

They talked. Maria cried harder. She listened for several minutes and then cried even more. The last thing I heard was "Señor Roberto will help. He is here and he is the one that found you. God be with you my niece. With hugs and kisses until very soon."

Maria turned towards me.

"The doctor has her Mexican passport and she cannot come home without it".

I wondered if she ever had a passport. Probably not. The people from the *pueblitos* are pretty invisible, even down here. They don't get passports.

"Lupe said she knew about you Señor Roberto and had seen your picture on Spanish television saving the boy. She said she trusts you. The TV said you were the gringo santo from Oaxaca."

Santo Gordo strikes again. This was beyond weird, it was insane. Weirdness just scared people but insanity made them laugh—that was much worse. Sometimes people died laughing.

The Señora came in from the street, banging the outside door. She called up to Lupe and me, probably noticing the wash sitting half done. Lupe and I walked on to the steps that overlooked the courtyard. Lupe called out in Spanish so fast that I could not understand anything. She ran down the steps and hugged the Señora. The Señora talked quietly to her. They were both crying. After a few minutes the Señora looked up at me.

"Good, you found her. Now what are you going to do?"

I stood silently. I had no answer.

"You will help? Señor Roberto." I was not sure if that was a question.

Why not, I thought. I was Santo Gordo. "Certainly," I said, "with the help of God."

Not the smartest thing I had ever said, but it was done.

I went back to my room and tried to let things sink in. They were happening too fast. Too many of them too.

I sat in front of the computer just staring out the window again, at the flowers, looking for a little peace, when I noticed an email on the screen. Another thing that I did not need.

I did not get many. I kept a low profile and tried to live without too much computer noise. Too much of any kind of noise. Maybe that was what Mexico was for me—a big filter to keep out the noise. Not many ads to see down here, not too much to buy, not too much news to read, a couple old Mexican movies for chilly nights, and some expat gossip on the roof every week or so and a dinner or two with Mexican friends when they had time. That was me. Twenty-first century noise-free.

I looked back at the computer. The email was from TreeGirl. It had my daughter's name in the title "A message from Rhonda." I opened it.

Father, I am contacting you because something has happened. Helen died yesterday. She did not want to tell you when she was sick, but I thought it only decent for you to know that she has passed. I was lucky to spend the last months with my mother in San Francisco. She will be cremated and the memorial is next week. You may come if you wish. Also, I now call myself Randy.

Jesus. It had been a long time. Helen had been the healthy one and I was always the one everyone said would drop dead soon, especially after my cancer. She was fit and climbed rocks and all that nature stuff. I sat around in the TV room. I figured she would live forever. I hadn't talked to her for seven years. I didn't have any contact. But I had lived twenty years with her and we raised a kid. Or maybe she was the one that raised her.

And Rhonda-Randy, what was she telling me in that formalese? I should go to the memorial? I think that was what she was saying.

I thought about Helen and Rhonda that night. I had not thought of Helen for a long time. That was a dead part of me. I still felt for Rhonda; I was afraid of her. I always felt like I had done something horribly wrong when I heard from her. But it was time to see if we could talk a little. She was older, I was much older. We would see.

Friday

Crepes Drowned in *Cajeta*

I got up and, first thing, bought the tickets for a Sunday flight–day after tomorrow. Randy sent me the date and location for the memorial, north of San Francisco on Monday. Nothing about where she lived. I did not pry. I would see her next week.

A lot to do before that though. I had to finish the report before I left. Otherwise Señor Licenciado Ruiz might think I was running away and God knows what would happen then. Probably never be able to get back in the country. Or worse, a couple bullet holes in my shirt to show in the *Sección Roja*.

I called Arturo at his work to say goodbye. He was surprised. I had not talked with him for a couple days. The truth was I was backing away from him. I was scared of involving him with Ruiz. I figured the gold mine would pollute the water somewhere and I did not want him involved. The mine looked like a high-level political deal not subject to review. I wanted to keep him and his noble water ideas and his family out of the intrigues because he could not do anything about it. Or maybe I just did not want him to know I was involved.

I had some time before my afternoon visit to Ruiz' office, so I decided to take a walk, a long one, just to clear my head. Things were piling up on me and a walk always helped. I planned to go from one end of the touristy pedestrian corridor to the other and maybe back. I started at the north end walking next to the fifteen-foot tall stone wall, my normal sun-avoiding path. A few late summer tourists looked up as they stood in the roadway studying the blocks in the wall, ones cut long ago by Indian stonemasons, chiseling by hand the green Oaxacan rock from the mountains near the city. I walked, hands in my pockets, trying to think of nothing, just watching the meandering mortar lines in the walls. These were not regimented European or American walls; they were forgiving Mexican ones that fitted together all sizes of stones surrounded by varying widths of mortar. These walls had survived three earthquakes while the newer squared off, right angle walls fell.

The wall, two blocks long, had no windows and only a single doorway cut into it. Family maids gathered around this door, wearing their aprons as uniforms so everyone knew they were working while they gossiped and made cell phone calls. They held snacks for their young charges, the students on the other side of the wall in school. A bell rang, the kind I remembered from my school days, and children came whooping and running through the door to make a quick grab of their maids' patiently held plastic containers and lunch boxes. Then the kids ran back inside, some with a quick hug for the maid.

I keep going. I wanted to remember this walk. I would not have many more before the flight to the States. And who knew what after that.

I walked near Ruiz' office. It was just off the pedestrian street. I speeded up to get beyond his building, looking everywhere but in its direction. I would go there later.

I passed two churches and the museum that was a convent until the Revolution. It was next to the big church, Santo Domingo, where I first ran into Ruiz. The grounds in front of its bell towers had been replanted a couple years back to be ecologically and anti-colonially correct. I looked at the all-Mexican agave plants that had replaced the years-old rows of European-imported roses. I missed the old plants, but the *conquista* European flowers had to go. Of course, they ended up in a politician's garden, so they did not go far.

I continued on, passing shops along the pedestrian corridor. I stopped briefly, adjusting my suspenders and hat and cleaning my sunglasses. I was next to a shop full of rugs, hand woven by some family a few miles away. The rugs sported Picasso and Miro designs. Someone convinced the local weavers that tourists did not want Zapotec Indian patterns. Maybe he was right, but the old geometric shapes worked a lot better on a loom than those free flowing, loose lined sketches that the Europeans made with their pencils and brushes. Rugs are made on squared-off wooden frames with shuttles going only back and forth. They cannot meander and float like a painter's brush. So the nudes all had what looked like chips on their shoulders and their curves looked like they were made with lego blocks. But I guess the rugs sold. They were always adding new ones.

Next door, a new import on the block had opened. The Cinnabun store with its buttery shopping mall smell was all wrong for Oaxaca. Things smelled spicy here. One or two tourists looked in, and then walked over to the mole restaurant next door. The big Oaxacan chocolate company ran that restaurant and always tempted me. Today I resisted and kept walking.

Next came tourist bars, still empty but thumping heavy metal even before lunch. I was getting near the end of the pedestrian corridor and ended my walk passing between the colonial buildings of the University on one side and the old city library on the other to reach my goal, the Zocalo.

I went into the square, past where the police barricade had been holding back teachers a week ago. Tourists arriving today had no idea what had happened. They thought they found a Mexican peace haven with everyone smiling, hugging, and back-patting. The strike did not leave many traces. Only a couple almost hidden graffiti scrawlings, not yet painted over, calling for assassinations and anarchy.

A waiter motioned me toward one of the café sidewalk tables. It was time to reward myself with coffee and a treat. I was back in my Oaxaca mood again as I ordered. Then when things arrived, I made my way through the goat-milk

Cajeta, a caramel sauce, covering a perfect crepe, drowning it and not gently. I chewed my sweet, drippy snack slowly and looked out at the Zocalo crowd. People wandered by as aimlessly as I was feeling. It was a good afternoon.

But it ended. As I was putting a tip on the table, Rob and Clara walked up. They caught me by surprise from the back. Otherwise I would have head-downed it and charged the other way. But they had me.

"Hola, Señor Roberto," Clara called out. She had already started Spanishing her talk.

"Hello, ¿*Como están*?" I Spanished her back with a smile.

I needed to figure out how to put it to them. I had to tell them that they were volunteering too hard. They needed to let their volunteering float up from the Mexicanos, not be rammed down by the tall white gringos with their funny ideas about how life must be lived or, even worse, from their duty to Americanize those less fortunate, the ones who did not live in the suburbs of el Norte.

"Really good, really good. Gracias." Clara was bubbling, bouncing up and down, wearing her new, long, embroidered *huipil*, a shift or tunic—I think that is what you would call it in English—that she probably bought in the mercado. It was a complex weaving of reds, greens, yellows and blues, something denied her in the States. I was sure of that.

"Thank you for getting us started here. We are having so much fun helping people."

"I am glad that you found the preschool." I smiled a big one for Clara.

"Oh you heard about it. I guess you hear everything when you live here." She looked like she was thinking about what it would be like living here all the time.

It was time for me to start explaining. "I know the preschool. It is a good one. All volunteers, no one pays anybody anything there."

"Isn't it a state school?" Rob spoke up. He was chewing on his thoughts about Oaxaca. He still wore his cargo shorts and Hawaiian shirt but had slathered on a lot of white sun screen. He looked like one of the dead sugar skulls that everyone Mexican puts on their altars.

"Sort of, but the local people are trying to make it better." I was not very clear. How do you explain the relationship between people and their government? Can you explain how the US works? I can't. But down here it is even trickier because I have to make a lot of guesses about the glue that holds everything together.

"We are just trying to teach these people a little responsibility about their buildings. They need to understand that a building needs to be maintained. Not let go, like the old walls and sidewalks everywhere." Rob was lecturing. He brought up the sidewalks. All tourists bring them up after they trip in a hole; then they want the Mexicans to fix everything. Sometimes I even want them to fix the holes, especially the one in the sidewalk by my front door.

"These people are very responsible, look at how they care for the old," I lectured back. "The children watch out for old parents and uncles and aunts. They walk them in the parks, dress them, take care of them even after they are dead." I was thinking of the Day of the Dead coming up soon when sugar skulls are everywhere and families sit around their ancestors' graves and offer mezcal and cigarettes and maybe a set of car keys to the spirits that come out that night. They do it every year to check in with all their dead relatives.

"Yes, maybe, but they need to take care the buildings. Not let the government take care of everything for them. You know– teach a man to fish and all that." Rob had started in on what was obviously his individualism creed that, I bet, was repeated over and over to anyone in range. "I think that their paying for the paint is a good way to start them out."

"But you have to remember that they are very poor folks here. Teach a man to fish when he does not have a hook and when the river is dried up; then he starves."

"Did you see all their fancy cars? How can you be poor with a new SUV?"

I don't think Rob was looking at the people near the preschool. He was probably worried about all the SUVs targeting him when he crossed the streets. You need to show respect and fear for the SUVs down here, just like you need to do for the rich.

"Well they could use some financial help." I offered. I was wimping out, but you can only do so much with these first timers.

"Everyone can use money," Rob finished, getting more curt. He knew what he wanted to think and didn't want any criticism. Not from me. I had gone native.

Clara tried to smooth things over. She was smiling a big silly smile like the one I had back when we started talking. "We just wanted to thank you again. We are really having fun helping these people and it feels really good to be here."

"We have to go." Rob ended it and turned. Clara waved at me as she followed him across the Zocalo.

A lot of the short term tourists have fun here. And the young artsy expats too. In lots of ways. Some drink, some do dope, some scrape paint and cook tuna fish, some chase the local girls, and some chase the guys too. But we older expats do not understand fun very well. I am not a fun guy.

The word "fun" makes it sound like a thing, something you can hold, something you toss around or maybe let your dog back home chew on. Fun sounds like something that you could sell in a gift box in the mall.

I like the Spanish word for enjoying yourself, *divertirse*. Stuff is not involved; it is pure doing, making a diversion from your tiredness and work. Diverting yourself from your normal day.

I am diverting myself from most of my life. Not doing fun like the younger gringos. We old expats are definitely not funners. We are friendly, we are cheery sometimes, we are even pleasantly passing time, like the Mexicans say– *pasandolo bien*, but fun is not a thing for us, like it is for Barbie-ized, computer gamers.

I was lecturing myself. I could not help it. I had gotten old, skeptical of everything and a little nasty. I have good walks and bad mystery novels. I am cynical about all the rest. But I could have hit Rob in the head back there. That would have been fun.

My lecture was over. It wore me out. I took a few deep breaths and looked up from my thoughts. The streets were getting too sunny for me to stand around. I needed to get to Señor Ruiz' and start working.

I walked the four blocks his office, went past the guard and said hello to Señorita Receptionista. She was wearing a new outfit, even tighter than the one from the day before. She probably sprayed it on. She was part of her boss's showcase, like the angels in the garden and the carved stone doorway. These things do not go together well for gringo eyes, but were a perfect matched set for Mexicanos trying to show off their power.

I sat down, started the computer and plugged away, writing for a couple hours to explain what Ruiz needed to do: find a reliable oversight group to monitor the restoration fund. I was sure Señor Ruiz would read my comment wondering who he could buy off. And they must say something about the indigenous people near the mine. Even if no one were near, the plan must explain how the mine would affect villages when the tailings piled up. And the plan should find an NGO to follow the ongoing work. I was sure Señor Ruiz would be calculating how big a donation was needed to stay on some green group's good list.

I had not checked to see if there actually were any villages near the mine site. This time I memorized the latitude and longitude and planned on looking it up when I got home.

That hardly hurt. I told Miss Receptionista where the file was and she started printing it. I waved goodbye and headed to the door. Job done. Ruiz could go make a killing with the mine. I was out of it, Not even a bystander.

Trout

I was on schedule. I called my taxista friend Efraím.

"I want to book your cab for a couple hours." I had plans for the late afternoon and they involved food.

"This is a busy time. It will cost you." Efraím was one of the few Mexicans who understood male gringo kidding around, like the joking I got from the expats. I think it was because he worked in the States so long before harvesting his savings and buying a cab and a house here. He did not retire like me; he still worked. His harvest did not include Social Security like mine did. But he loved driving and would do it until he dropped dead at the wheel. I kidded him about that.

I met him five years back when he drove me from the airport. He talked a lot. He liked to think he was the silent Mexican type and I let him pretend. He told stories about

Oaxaca, but kept quiet about his family, come to think of it. We met mostly on the streets and in restaurants.

After a couple years I found out his children were grown and stayed on in el Norte, in Texas, when he returned here. Maybe his wife Lucia told me that. I did not see her much but when I did she was always waiting for some grandson or granddaughter to show up. She stayed at home and cooked most of the time, that was what Efraím told me. She kept her altar. She prayed. I think her time in the north isolated her. Efraím left the house to work; she locked herself in. He learned English; she just practiced Hail Marys. But now she would talk to me, happy that Efraím had a friend who came from the States, up where her grandchildren lived, the ones she always wanted to visit.

Efraím never talked much about his family's village either, out where his parents and the rest of his relatives lived. Their pueblo was in the south, a couple hours away, far enough away for a returnee who had learned our more solitary, independent gringo ways.

Efraím kept me up on the street knowledge of Oaxaca. He was not shut in an office; he saw what happened at street level. And he was open with me about Oaxaca and its politics and government, something I valued in this country where deference to the invader was the safest way to live. And we gringos were seen as the latest invaders, along with the *Chilangos*, the people from Mexico City, who had been flocking here and buying up property now that the new freeway made Oaxaca a rich man's weekend retreat.

"I will be there in five minutes." Efraím was always five minutes away, no matter how long it took to get there. So I sat on a bench and watched the street while I waited.

A food stand just down the block was busy. A woman in a turquoise apron was cooking on a *comal*, a big round metal sheet, lying on a charcoal burner. It blocked most of the smoke as she covered it with stuffed tortillas. A line of people, workers from nearby, waited for their food and sat on little wooden chairs when it arrived. There was a bucket for washing the plates when they finished. A couple scruffy dogs stood by waiting for scraps. The food smell started me thinking even more about comida. That was where I was heading with Efraím. He talked best when food was involved.

Ten minutes later a taxi pulled up and Efraím waved. I hopped in the front, "I'm ready to eat. How about you?"

"I want to eat, but so does my big family. I eat in the cab while I am driving and making money."

"But today it's on me. Drive me to that Angus place you know about. The one with steaks that get massaged before they slice them off the cow."

"I don't know. That place was not so good last time. Now I hear that their meat comes from a feed lot where they turn cattle into gringo meat to ship up north. That restaurant quit serving our proud Mexican *toros* that graze with their horns held high."

Efraím looked offended by the thought. Then he laughed.

"Now they buy steers that suffered a short penned-up life and ended with a long truck trip, a whack on the head and a deep sleep in a deep freeze, like the one the Policía has in the morgue by the river."

I was not sure where this conversation was going, but I was no longer in charge. Efraím usually had only one requirement for his meat–dead. Today he was leading me somewhere.

He continued, "I know a place. A mountain stream where giant trout jump and swim and grow in tanks filled with water running down from the Sierra Madre. They have one for you right now, laughing and smiling and not knowing its afternoon fate."

All this to get me to the Trout Farm restaurant, but that was ok with me. I liked the place. After all those moles and meats and sauces and heavy meals, maybe it was time for a healthy change. "Fish it is. Let's go."

"Today, I will give you the special cab rate, if I get a little fish bribe to keep the price down."

Efraím always charged the same, fifteen dollars an hour for long trips. I always paid it because I knew he could not afford to take off from work, even to be with friends. The money had to come in for supporting his family, his parents and old aunts and uncles that he left in his pueblo somewhere up in the mountains after everyone young headed to el Norte or Mexico City for work.

There was not much work in Oaxaca, unless you started your own business, like Efraím did with the cab. If you had a window on the street you opened a *Miscelánea* store selling soft drinks and candy. If you had nothing you cleaned car windows with old newspapers on street corners. If you were lucky and had some money, then a cab was a good investment, especially if you knew someone and could get a permit. Entrepreneurship was not some fancy business school word down here, it was survival.

I wondered how, in this web of small-time businesses, they did not get in each other's way. I suggested Adam Smith's invisible hand to Efraím, the hand that the US worshiped like an old saint's relic.

"No, it is the fat hand of the cops who run things. Señor Collecta comes by every week for his cut and you better have the cash ready. That is how things are organized here. I am sure you have fat hands up in the States as well."

It seemed like there was a fat hand scandal every couple weeks back in the States, but somehow we pretended it did not happen. Or we did so until recently when the fat cats took way too much. My mind was wandering, thinking about cats and fish as Efraím made it through the city streets and we went north out on the highway towards the Trout Farm. It was something of a secret place. Not many tourists knew about it. That was one of the joys of living here; you knew stuff that was not in the guide books. Maybe knew too much.

But I had to stop thinking about fish. It was time get down to business.

"Efraím, I need your help on something small." I did not want him to think I was asking for help with the Colonel. That was too big a thing to ask anyone who had to live here. Instead I asked if he knew the preschool in the colonia by the river. The one where Rob and Clara were making life better for those poor Mexicans.

"I need you to buy some things and deliver them to the school. Ten cans of tuna fish, Chicken of the Sea, yes, like a chicken that lays eggs, a couple boxes of Kraft macaroni. Kraft, it's from the States and you can get it all at the Walmart near the airport.

When Efraím was in the States, even for a long time, I think he bought food at the Mexican stores getting ten pound bags of beans and premade tortillas, maybe cans of *menudo* or *mole*, but not Chicken of the Sea. I knew my volunteer Clara would not settle for a Mexican brand. I also asked for a couple gallons of paint. Pink would be good. Just tell them at the preschool that God provides. Don't mention me."

"They will know it is you. Who else would buy pasta in a box at the Walmart but a gringo? And Chicken Tuna. The story of El Santo Gordo will grow; I am sure, after this."

I did not know what else to do. I had given my word to straighten out the volunteer mess and money seemed the easiest way to settle things before I flew off. I gave Efraím two thousand pesos. I wanted enough left over to make him happy. He took it and understood the change was for his time.

"I will do it tomorrow, Señor General." He saluted.

Efraím now had to pay attention to driving. People were running like chickens across the road at the bus stop ahead. Above the roadway, concrete pedestrian bridges had been built but everyone just ran through the lanes of cars. The concrete was not for the people anyway; it was for the contractors to make money.

I remembered back when they were building like crazy when I was young, all around Baltimore. Concrete got poured everywhere when they built the freeways. Lots of land opened up for development and our old Vice President, the Greek guy, who got kicked out by Nixon–Can you believe it, too criminal for Nixon–he was in charge of north Baltimore's development back then. They say that was why the towns got so screwed up: no roads, no parks, no schools. The story was he had a fat hand but took tiny bribes, was too easy to buy, not like in the well planned areas near DC where big corporations handled everything. That was the normal way things worked in the US with greased palms that the lawyers made legal. No one got in trouble and great things happened. Like our freeway system. Efraím was right. We do things big up north.

We were passing a jumble of low block buildings and small businesses: *Rosterias* grilling chicken, muffler shops pounding away, tiny grocery stores, even an adobe brick factory where men in straw hats dug clay out of the riverbank and dried it in the sun. There was no zoning on the highway outside of the Oaxaca. Zoning was not an Oaxacan concept. They have historical districts in the center that you cannot change from the way they looked in the 19th century but everything outside of the district was fair game. You could do anything, if you paid the right person. And in the historical district too, if you paid enough.

Every once and a while we passed a motel, usually with wrought iron gates and heavy curtains covering its garage, so you saw none of the cars parked inside. They were for sneak-away couples to do a special comida or maybe even nights. The type of place Señorita Receptionista would go with her boss.

We went about ten miles, past the big cement statue of Benito Juarez, the only Indian president of Mexico, the one who made Mexico a real country.

"You know what is wrong with your country," Efraím started the conversation.

"You do not have great American villains in your history. Your villains are all from other countries, except for your Mister Nixon. You started off by hating King George of England and now you hate Hitler and bin Laden. And don't forget your Texans hate our Santa Ana. On the other hand, we have wonderful Mexican villains, they stole, they pillaged, they led our country. We hate them all; we love them all. Except, of course, for Benito. He was pure, like you think your Lincoln was.

Efraím read history. When he sat waiting in the cab he always had a book open. He knew more than most professors. But he was a practical political scientist who interpreted what happened from a cab driver's level. To him George Washington splashed mud on the people when he rode by after a rain, just like the Russians did when they drove through with their tanks. You needed that kind of attitude down here. Everything was suspect, past and present. Maybe it was something that we needed more up north, especially about our past.

"Was the dead Colonel one of the villains?" I asked. Efraím had given me an opening to start talking about the assassination.

"He was so bad that he made most of our villains look like saints. Our villains have a loving streak, like our mountains have a vein of gold buried deep inside. But the Colonel only had a streak of *mierda* running though him."

Somehow, this got me going. I started talking and could not stop. I explained how Señor Ruiz approached me in the restaurant and then about the report and finally the gold mine. Efraím was a good listener. He kept shaking his head.

"So now you have mud on you? The gringos like to think they can stay clean in this world. But that is the choice, live muddy or die. Or go home."

I did not like the second alternative. The one that ended up in the *Sección Roja*. And the third one was not so good either.

We started climbing up the Sierras. The restaurant was up about eight thousand feet, looking over the valley. Efraím drove the twisting two lanes, honking at tight corners making sure any big semis coming down would not accidently crush us.

I looked back. The Oaxaca valley, maybe 30 miles across, was hemmed in with mountains. Brown smog sat over the city. It was a recent addition, not there five years ago.

We climbed higher and passed through the first clouds hanging on the slopes and entered a scraggly pine forest. The air was cool and damp and my skin opened up and breathed a little after fighting the dry afternoon sun on the valley floor.

We came up behind an old school bus carrying its load of passengers out to their mountain villages. The Mexican red, white and green trinity of colors was carefully painted over the buses' dents and bent panels.

Efraím looked at me, smiled, crossed himself and then pulled out to pass on a steep curve. There was nothing but curves on this road. He laughed. "I always peek ahead and know what is coming." It was true you could see the road as it curved up ahead. It was visible, at least partly, around every bend. "Besides I am psychic about oncoming cars. I can feel them here." He tapped his chest. I wanted to grab the wheel from him but instead clumsily crossed myself. I called on any Virgin to help, like a good Mexican would, and hoped the Señora's blessings were still in effect.

Finally after climbing for a half hour, we reached a dirt turnout leading to a brick building held secure by a dozen hand-poured cement columns. Steel rebar rods stuck out the roof, capped with beer and coke bottles, waiting for the owner to get enough money to add a second floor, like in most of the country houses out here. This house sat directly on the rock face of the mountain. It jutted out about twenty feet over a ledge, with a free hanging terrace looking down on the steep mountainside. Lights and plastic flags were strung over tables on the terrace, letting everyone know it was a restaurant. It had a great view. You could swan dive four or five hundred feet before hitting rock. Vultures and hawks circled below, far down the mountain waiting for someone to slip.

The restaurant looked closed. I did not see anyone. A family lived here, the owners, so I knew someone was inside. You never leave a building completely empty here in the countryside. After we yelled for a few minutes, a woman came out.

"We are closed. The fish died. We have nothing today."

Efraím tried talking with the woman. She just repeated that the fish had died. I walked over and looked. The tanks were empty. Fish were piled on the ground. They dead-eyed me as I walked around. Stream water flowed by the tanks, looking different, not the clear water from my last visit–it was cloudy and had something that looked like soap scum lining the banks.

"Someone dumped something into the stream." I yelled over to Efraím. A couple thousand feet of mountain were above us. Lots of room to get rid of poisons from a factory.

I was angry. The worst thing was that I couldn't do much about it. Probably someone with the government or with someone with a lot of pull did this. Or got their workers to do it.

Mexico talks green. Arturo tells me things are getting better. But this was a mess. Maybe I was feeling guilty about Ruiz' gold mine, or maybe I was still thinking about the mountains in Appalachia that died for their coal. But I wanted to do something about my fish stream. About my fish restaurant. About my lunch.

"We need to find out what happened," I yelled to Efraím as I was walking back to the front of the restaurant.

He turned to me. He had been talking more with the woman. "Her husband already went up the mountain. He took his rifle and his friends. We probably should stay away."

"Let's just drive by."

"OK, but no stopping," Efraím warned. I think he was wondering what happened too, or I would not have talked him into it.

We headed up the road. Efraím drove slower than before. We climbed about a half mile and then saw a couple of old pickup trucks parked on the side.

The owner of the restaurant was climbing into one of them. He was yelling to the others who were running out from an old gate at the side of the road. Efraím and I passed them. Looking back in the mirror I could see the trucks pulling out as fast as their thirty or forty year old engines could go.

Efraím said "We keep going." We climbed for five minutes and got to a point where we could see down the slope. I climbed out and looked. In the clearing below I saw a shanty and some rudimentary water channels built along the stream. Paper bags, ripped open and dumped, were piled on something white and powdery. It was everywhere.

And a body lay beside the stream.

"Time to go home. That's it. We can read about this tomorrow." Efraím called as he headed back to the cab. I took a last look.

Efraím set records going down the hill, lurching into curves blessing himself way too many times, telling me that one assassination was all that you are allowed in this life and I should stop this sort of thing.

Another coincidence, I was thinking when Efraím said, "You know God arranges coincidences. Life is not just a roll of the dice. You need to be careful because things like this come in threes. Like the Holy Trinity." He didn't say that I could be number three, the holy ghost of the group, but we were both thinking it.

He dropped me off. "We will talk later about Señor Ruiz and his gold mine. That isn't the big problem now. Just keep quiet about the dead fish and their dead friend."

I spent another evening hiding out in the apartment. It was like old times. I ate a hot dog left in the refrigerator and had a can of beer. I slept some that evening. It was hot in the apartment but the heat didn't keep me awake. It was my brain going in circles that kept me pacing around the room. I was waiting to see the paper the next morning to figure things out.

Saturday

Picnic

I did not have to look in the newspaper's *Sección Roja*. The story was on the front cover. A picture showed the body, lying just as I had seen it yesterday. The headline proclaimed "Murder for Gold."

Wait a minute–it was murder for fish, not gold.

I tried to look uninterested as I bought a paper and headed to La Avenida for my morning start.

Carlos was there. Lance too. The whole gang was sitting around. Must have been something going on. Not like July 4th a year before, I hoped. I forgot it that year and they never stopped reminding me till after Christmas.

"Hey Roberto, you are off the front page," Carlos yelled to me. I walked over.

"Can you believe it, gold?" Lance chimed in. "But it was just an old played-out mine up in the hills. It didn't have enough for anyone but a desperate farmer to try. They say there was no possibility that he found enough to even enough to buy his beans and rice."

"A thousand dollars an ounce buys a lot of beans." Old Carlos always had an answer.

I played dumb and asked what happened. They explained someone was robbed or maybe he had partners who fought and one man was killed with a machete. There was no talk about the dead fish, so I said nothing.

I sipped my espresso and ordered a couple Mexican sweet rolls. One was bright pink and the other yellow. This was Mexico, after all, and those were the choices. I could only grieve for the fish for so long. And I was trying to forget the dead man.

The expats went on and on and I listened. They only knew what was in the paper and made it last about an hour with lots of speculation about everyone. The dead Colonel came up a couple times and people looked my way. I shrugged my shoulders. The talkers kept going. Then someone yelled and a van pulled up.

"Roberto, are you coming?"

"I have to get ready to go back to the States, sorry." They wanted to ask me why I was heading back, but the driver was honking. I did not know where they were heading but they were carrying a lot of beer and mezcal. They got in and the van pulled out probably for one of the lakes or other cooler places that the group liked for parties up the mountain.

Another horn started honking, a cab. Efraím wanted me. I took my last sip and climbed in with him.

"Free ride today. Let's talk," he started out. "We did not go to the Trout Farm yesterday. We went to visit my family up in the mountains."

"I knew we did something like that. I am not stupid."

"You gringos are like rich card players who talk all the time and give away what you are holding. You don't care because you are rich and winning one hand does not matter. We are silent because we know we cannot lose, even one hand."

Efraím played a lot of cards up in the States. I think his winnings helped pay for the cab.

"I am learning silence," I said. "Now that I met the Colonel and Señor Ruiz, I am learning to be quiet. But everyone is talking about gold."

"There you go. Talking about gold is not being quiet. I think that this time the police will not be so generous questioning you. You know the law is different down here. You are guilty until you prove yourself innocent. That was thanks to Mr. Napoleon, who left us his version of justice."

Everything had a historical reference with Efraím. But I knew how difficult it was if you got accused here. Everyone kept quiet to make sure the finger of the law pointed at someone else.

"The first time you got off easy because you are a gringo and everyone knew who really killed the Colonel. This time, up in the hills, the police will be trying to get a killer for a good newspaper photo. They love those shots with the cops wearing ski masks and the *ladrón*, the thief, looking confused, tired and ready to confess to anything."

"Did they question the fish restaurant family?"

"What restaurant family? I do not remember them at all and you shouldn't either. You still have much to learn to be a Mexicano. At least a poor one like me."

A call came in for the taxi on his radio. Efraím was needed on the other side of the Zocalo.

"Adios, Roberto, mi amigo, remember–silence is golden. My English teacher in Texas taught me that when I was learning to espeek."

I hopped out and waved as the taxi sped off. He had learned to play gringo much better than I had learned to be Mexicano. Quiet is unnatural to gringos, like holding a rock and not throwing it at something. But I was working on it.

I still needed to pack and to get a place to stay in California tomorrow.

It was August and San Francisco would be cold, but north of the city, the temperature goes to a hundred plus. Packing required some thought. I used to just dump the dresser drawers into the suitcase. If the airlines took it, then I took it. That was my packing. Then the airlines quit taking, at least for free, and my hundred pounds of luggage got slimmed down to twenty in a carry-on. So that afternoon I had to pack for real. And what do I wear to a California memorial for a Wiccan ex-wife anyway. Not a suit and tie, I bet.

I was trying to decide whether to take my computer when Señora Concepcion called up to me.

"Señor Roberto, gracias. We have discovered that you are going to California to rescue our Lupe."

She came up and hugged me and then Maria followed and she hugged me and they both were crying. I was trapped on the stairs outside my room.

"You are partly right, I have to go to California, but it is personal business."

"And you will rescue Lupe after that." Her voice had turned into a command.

"And then…" I tried to be non committal, but standing unbalanced on the stairs with two large women leaning on me and no handrails to save me from a ten foot drop. I added, "OK."

OK was enough for them. OK was legally binding, a never-to-be-broken contract for them. They went back to tears and hugs.

I guess I could drive back to Merced next week, see Lupe and catch a flight out later. It was not that far. I could meet with Lupe. Sure.

Sunday

Cold Turkey Sandwich

Efraím drove me out to the airport for the 10 AM flight on Sunday. We did not talk much. He reminded me about silence. Then I got out at the Oaxaca airport.

They wanted you two hours early according to the ticket, but it only took twenty minutes to get processed so half the people came late and almost missed the plane. Luckily the plane was always a little late too.

The airport was old fashioned. It reminded me of one I went to as a kid, where I flew my model airplanes on an old runway left over from WWII. It had that same feel here, like you should have a picnic at the end of the runway and wave to the pilots sticking their heads out the window when they landed.

There were no ramps to the flights from the terminal. You walked out to a roll-up stairway. When you looked back from it, you could see families waving goodbye at the terminal windows over the gate. The airport used to let visitors on the outside balcony, but those days ended with all the new gringo-led security. Everything got hand searched now, but the Mexican security teams helped you. They picked up and opened bags, they repacked for you, and sometimes they just chatted a while.

Best of all when you walked out behind the plane to board, you were not in some metal tube; you could look up at the mountain sky waiting for you to take off.

My jet came in and did a fancy, non-stop u-turn to circle back to the terminal. This was not a complicated airport. It had one runway and a taxi strip from the middle of the runway to the terminal—that was it. We boarded and I squeezed into a seat about the same size as on the buses here. Then the plane went to the other end of the runway, did another U-turn and we were off.

In a half hour I started seeing signs of Mexico City sprawl. Ten minutes more and I could smell the city. I watched skyscrapers fly by out my window. We went lower and it seemed like we were landing in the middle of an apartment complex, but just at the last minute the runway started and we touched down.

The Mexico City terminal building was a straight, a mile-long hall, paralleling the runway with gates every 25 yards or so. It was not one of those grape-cluster designs, like most airports have these days. The new designs required up front planning. This airport looked like it just got added on to, getting longer and longer. There was no planning, just getting bigger, like something alive and needing more and more room.

I got my exercise walking from domestic on one end to international on the other. My walk was crowded by Mexican businessmen in suits and ties pulling out cell phones and looking serious, talking deals and money. In Oaxaca it was different. Everyone with cell phones just called their girlfriend or boyfriend or maybe their mother.

I finally reached my gate for the US flight and saw the last of the summer tourists finishing up their week or, if lucky, their month of vacation, sitting around pecking at computers, doing final emails and waiting for the plane to load.

We flew four hours up the coast and landed at SFO with a wonderfully boring flight. The only thing interesting was the cold turkey sandwich that cost eight dollars. Actually it wasn't interesting, but it was all I had that day.

I headed straight to passport control where the lines were not too jammed. Only one big jet besides us, a 747 from China, had landed in the past hour. I smiled at the young immigration officer and handed over my passport. He sat behind the counter with his digital camera, computer, new thumbprint machine and some other electronic boxes. I was wondering if he had a gun or whether it was something electronic too.

He looked at my picture, scanned my passport and started typing.

"Where have you been sir?

"Mexico."

Anywhere else, sir? How long were you there, sir?

"No, nowhere else and eight months down there this time." I hated their sir talk. Sirs were tacked on every sentence like a little kick in the pants.

I felt a tap on my shoulder. "Can you come with me for a moment, sir?"

"I am in the middle of getting my passport checked." I turned and it was another immigration official and he was not smiling.

"Come with me." It was an order and he did not end it with sir.

———

"And you mean to tell us that an associate of one of the drug kingpins in Mexico just let you take care of his son while you were riding around."

"I was not taking care of him. I was not riding around. I was walking by. Then someone shot him. If I were taking care of the boy, they probably would have shot me too when they got the Colonel.

"So you knew the Colonel?"

"Everyone in Oaxaca tells me he was a Colonel. I don't know who he was."

I was trying to figure out what happened. They picked me. It never had happened before. They wanted me and they knew about the Colonel.

I was running over the possibilities and I remembered the face recognition article I read a while back. I bet that was what it was. They had the picture from the paper of me and the boy and when I walked into immigration, some computer looked at my short hair and white beard and pink face and nailed me. This was the police of the future. And it had me in the present.

I had been sitting in the room for three hours. They accused me of everything they could think of. I had no idea what they were talking about. Then they left me alone to stew. It was getting late, but I didn't have anything to do until the next day. If they fed me, then this was just another day. A little confined, maybe, but air conditioned and not too uncomfortable.

I was trying to keep from being bored. Nothing to do but contemplate my sins, I guess. I started counting the panels in the ceiling, then tiles on the floor. Official buildings could be awfully boring in the States, not like old haciendas turned in to offices in Mexico. In Ruiz' office I could look at the angel statues out the window. Even in the police station there was an old stone wall to look at. Here there was not much. Maybe that was their plan. Bore a confession out of me.

Everything was grey and started melting into one another. No style, no pride, as we say in Mexico. Efraím would have been proud of me, Señor Ruiz, too.

I was trying not to think about what was going on the other side of the grey wall. They were probably checking everything in my life. Ruiz had checked me out, why not the other side.

The door opened.

"I see you are making yourself at home, Mr. Evans. Most of our visitors are a bit more concerned when they come in here."

I sat up straighter. "I have done nothing. I just had the bad luck to walk by a shooting. I did not know anyone there." I had decided to be quiet about Señor Ruiz.

"Have you been approached by any associates of the Colonel after the shooting?

"No." I tried to sound convincing but my voice cracked.

"They are thorough, these drug gangs, and would check if you were involved. Since you are alive, I assume that they decided you were not part of the assassination. But has anyone contacted you?

"Not really, someone from the government talked to me. That was all." I decided to leave out the story about the first gold mine and Señor Ruiz and the other gold mine and the dead man on the mountain.

"Are you sure? " I never was good at holding back, either talking or eating, but I was biting my tongue just then. Silence is golden, even outside of Mexico.

"We are almost ready to believe you. I want you to think about what you told us. Here is my card." I read it– Inspector Norton of the DEA. "You call me if you hear from anyone. Do you understand?"

This sounded exactly like a TV show. Most of what I knew about crime came from TV and my mystery books. I was surprised when real life sounded the same. These cops probably learned their scripts from the same shows I watched.

I had gone through interrogations twice now, once English, once Spanish. I liked Spanish better. They were both like TV shows, but in English it was missing all the long polite sentences that Spanish actors managed to get out of the detectives' mouths when the shows were dubbed in Mexico.

"Do you think I am in danger?" I was still checking with anyone who might know what was really going on.

"If you were in danger, then I would not be seeing you right now. Danger like that, it does not last long. You would be very dead."

Everyone was always so reassuring.

I hoped this was the last detective scene for me for a while. I was ready for a happy ending, but I had suspicions that this mystery might drag out on a bit longer.

He said I could go. My things were there in a pile. Someone had gone through everything. They had not cut anything open but I was guessing my clothes were radioactive after all the X-ray inspections. I wondered what they thought I was bringing in. Drugs? Money? Do they carry the money from Mexico? I read in the newspapers– guns go south, drugs go north and money goes everywhere.

I had a clean conscience, but that only helps at confession with a priest, not when the DEA was going through your life. They figured no police record means you are good, a pro, because no one caught you before. I learned that from TV too.

I repacked my stuff, got my rental car and checked in at one of the hotels by the airport. The room was air conditioned, smelled like disinfectant and the windows would not open. Good to be home in the States.

I did all the things you do when you come back from Mexico. I showered fifteen minutes with no worries about using up all the water. I brushed my teeth out of the tap and didn't even think of germs. I threw toilet paper into the john and watched it zip away when I pulled the handle. The Mexican toilet paper taboo is the first thing that everyone asks about down there. Is Mexican plumbing really so bad that you cannot put TP in the john? Every Mexican believes it like they do the Virgin birth. We gringos are not such good believers. If the paper goes then all is fine, but if something clogs up then we start to believe. That is the American way. We have faith, but we verify.

In Mexico they have TV, internet, smartphones, skateboards, California cuisine, and rock concerts, but their water and sewer lines remind you that they are not far that from the middle ages in some things. A lot of people come back to the States just to have clean water, hot showers and toilets that work, the real basics of life, the true American dream.

I lay down and quit thinking about the bathroom. I needed to plan the next day. I had not seen my daughter for five years and I had quit thinking about my wife a long time before that.

In the motel, back in the States again, I started remembering how my wife and I met young. We were wide-eyed and ready to help the world love dolphins and gorillas and put windmills and bicycles everywhere. We were Earth Day babies, naïve starting out, but changing over time. I guess this happened to lots of people. She stayed home with the baby at first and then after ten years of not much to do began the country club martini route. Then she went womans rights. I went to work, made money and was good at it. Not good at money, but good at work, developing open pit mines.

The trouble with the world is that it feels good to do something, no matter what. And it feels even better if you do it well. I expect the guy who pushes the button on the electric chair feels great when it works. We are wired to do stuff and feel good when it's over. Then when you retire or get fired, then you have time to think about what you did. And wish you didn't.

Helen never understood why I was at work so much back then. She did not know what I did. Rhonda did know and thought I was the devil incarnate, off measuring mountains to turn into hell pits or locked up in my office tower late every night plotting some evil or another. I probably was.

Maybe Rhonda has changed. Maybe I have. We will see tomorrow.

Monday

Burgers

The drive up to Petaluma was easy. Everyone else was coming in to San Francisco that morning and I was going out. I drove through the valleys north of the city and up the freeway past the grass covered hills. The signs called them mountains, but they were not like Mexico mountains. These were just hills trying to make something of themselves. Sounds right for California.

Petaluma was where I was heading. It had become a boutique town. Its history as a chicken growing center was now just part of a new tourist marketing plan. Antique stores had chicken hatchers or whatever those things are called on display in the front windows. There was a chicken festival with someone dressed up, covered in feathers, running around and dropping candy eggs.

The town had gone Italian too. I guess because it was at the edge of wine country. I had a quick lunch in a place that had suburban teenagers trying to pull off "a my name is Pasquale" waiter routine. Bread was dipped in oil, not buttered. Spaghetti was pasta. And sales of expensive wine paid the bills for a fancy interior decorator. The meal was good, though. I am not complaining. Well, not really. I remember when I used to eat around here forty years ago and could only get the meatloaf special with canned green beans. Big changes are not always bad. Or maybe I mean they are not completely bad.

The memorial was at a place called The Ranch. It was up a dirt road and had signs showing kids petting goats and cows. A non-profit vegan ranch, it proclaimed. They raised livestock but only to love. And to show kids that cows are people too. Why not?

Signs showed me where to park. I headed up a trail to the memorial. Women walked by wearing long dresses and sun hats. Men had beards and sandals. I would fit in.

The service had just started. Rhonda was talking. She saw me, paused, nodded, and continued. She finished and others got up to talk. Helen was a wonderful woman, everyone agreed. I stood in the back and listened. Most of the things they talked about happened after we split up. A youngish couple carrying guitars walked to the front and the whole group sang songs that I did not recognize. Someone handed out the words. Then Rhonda picked up a small plain box, Helen's ashes, and she walked through the woods dropping some here and some there, like Johnny Appleseed. People were crying.

I was feeling distant. I was sure these were nice people; they looked a lot like the Type Ones I knew down in

Oaxaca, but I had no idea who they were. Just like I had no idea what Helen was really like. But today I was going to know more about Rhonda, I mean Randy.

I stayed behind as people walked out of the woods talking in groups. I watched Randy hugging everyone and getting whispers of encouragement. After an hour or so of saying goodbye, everyone started leaving. Randy came over to where I was standing under a group of tall eucalyptus trees in the shade.

"Thank you for coming." She looked older. She was older, of course. She had that serious look, almost comical, the one she had all the way through high school and probably through college. I must have looked serious too. Neither of us knew quite what to do.

I did not want to be her enemy—that was certain—but I had no idea what I wanted to be. She was part of me, the blood part, but I had let everything dry up. That happened when I was in shock from the divorce and when Rhonda called me a criminal and said she never wanted to see me again.

"Thank you for telling me about your mother's memorial." I started out.

"You should know about it." This was no touchie-feelie reunion. We were both staking positions. I was waiting for the artillery exchange, like the old days.

"Can I ride back with you?" That was a surprise. But I liked the idea because we would have a lot of time to sit next to each other. We might even say something.

We walked to the car. I opened it for her. She always said I was too courteous, like some old plantation owner.

"Remember, I am old fashioned," I said. She smiled for the first time and got in.

We drove off silently.

After getting on the freeway, I did my bit. I had rehearsed my line all the way up to Petaluma. It was honest, but honed after an hour of practice. "I want to tell you that I am proud of you. You are doing what you think is right and trying to make this world a better place. I respect you for that. I always have." I stretched it on the last part. When she threw rocks at my coal company windows during a demonstration, I was not feeling respect then. But looking back, maybe I did respect her for her rock throwing.

She looked at me. "I am not going to blame you for everything wrong in the world like I used to. You are just part of a system. Like I am. If I have children they will see my mistakes. I do not want to go over old ground. I want to see what we have in common. Maybe I only wanted to see if you were still alive."

I guess honesty is the best policy, but some manners never hurt. I don't know why she never learned any. She was no sweet talker.

I was quiet a minute. Glib stories about life in Mexico were not the thing to keep conversation flowing. A couple miles went by. All I could think to say was, "You look good. Healthy."

At this rate we would not even have a page of dialog done by the time we got back. And I did not know where back was. I started out the conversation again, "How are you, I mean really, how is your life going?"

She let go a little. "I am OK. I teach. I write. I have a friend. We are serious but not ready. We live together but not really. He is off in Africa writing about child soldiers. How about you?"

That was a lot in one mouthful. It was my turn. I was even shorter in the explanation of my life.

"I just do the day to day. Oaxaca is easy. I read. I walk. I know some expats and some Mexicans. No one special." Short and to the point.

But I kept going, "What do you teach?"

"In the Environment and Literature Program at a small college here in the city. I wake up people about the world and help them write about it. Most of them wanted to write about growing up hurt and unloved in the suburbs until they got to me. I like the work. I make them good students. A few become good writers. All of them change. "

"Do you live in the city?"

"Oh, you need to know where we are going. The Mission."

I remembered the Mission district from my time at grad school out here. The sunny part of the city, but the part that used to have heroin and gangs when I was there a long time back.

We were almost conversing normally about happenings and actions, not feelings. I wanted to leave feelings alone. Never scratch scabs. My mother told me that.

"I remember the Mission. Is it safe there now?" I was being the protective father.

"Don't worry, I like it." The pitch of her voice had jumped a half octave. She never wanted questions about her choices. I backed off and was quiet.

"Are you going back to Mexico soon?"

I decided to tell her about Lupe and my upcoming trip to Merced. Maybe news about me playing Santo Gordo in Mexico could help her see me differently. I told the Lupe story to help balance out my evil deeds portfolio. I left out the part about the assassination and the dead gold miner.

"I know about conditions for the undocumented. I teach them, too. Does Lupe know you are coming? What are you going to do when you see her?"

My girl always was a planner. I realized I had not thought much about what would happen when I got to Lupe. I was playing it by ear, or maybe just avoiding the whole thing. My focus was on making the Señora happy, I hadn't thought much about Lupe. I didn't know what I would do there.

Randy looked incredulous. "And you don't know what you will do? You do speak Spanish don't you?" That sounded like the old Randy letting her dad know exactly what she was thinking.

She continued, "You are a man. Do you think she is will trust you?"

So I told Randy about the assassination and the newspaper picture that Lupe and everyone in Mexico had seen.

"And you were worried about me living in the Mission? We might have some drive-bys but not real big-time assassinations."

"I am sure we both will be OK." I was proposing a treaty with Randy. You do your life; I will do mine.

That was when Randy pointed out we were being followed.

"You get used to that sort of thing when you are leading protests. You always are looking over your shoulder."

"Are they yours? Are they following you?" I asked.

"Who knows? Let's get rid of them." She started giving orders telling me where to turn. I took an exit in the northern part of San Francisco, just past the Golden Gate Bridge. We drove through the old military base and finally into a residential area near the ocean. She kept an eye on the sedan about five cars back. We drove city streets with her giving me turns and places to cut in and out. She waited until the last minute and told me to turn hard into a parking garage that was under an office supply store. Randy jumped out and headed for the stairs. We cut through the store, and then out a rear exit. I was panting. We walked a block on a side street and caught the Number 2 bus heading downtown. We were clear.

My head was spinning. I needed to fess up. I told her about the airport questioning and warned that the government might be following me—not the gang from the shooting in Mexico—at least that was what I hoped. Everyone said the Mexicans would have done me in a long time ago if they wanted to. This must be the feds, the DEA. She looked at me like I was crazy.

"Are you involved in anything down there? I am staying out of anything that can affect my work or my students."

"No, I swear. It was a coincidence. I just walked into it."

She shook her head. "Well I am going home."

"What about my car?"

"It's a rental, right? The company will come get it. Just call them. You can get around fine on a bus."

"But I don't care if the government follows me. I didn't do anything. I am just an innocent guy."

"And what am I? Do I look guilty? You think they were following me?" She was not quite yelling, but it was loud.

This was going downhill. I took my normal way out of a messy situation. "It is getting late. You must be hungry. Is the all night diner still in this block? Let's eat something."

She cooled down. As we ate through a veggie burger for her and a beef one for me, I think I convinced her I was not doing anything criminal. We finished eating and she looked over at me.

"You are going to need help with Lupe. She deserves real help and I am not busy right now. I will go down to Merced with you. Are you going tomorrow?"

I let the 'real help' remark slide. I knew Randy could pull this off better than I could. I would drive. And I would give Randy credit when I got back to see the Señora.

We were starting the first Roberto and Randy adventure–Saving Lupe.

We rode the bus to the subway station. She caught a train to the Mission district. I decided to just go back for the car. I did not care if anyone followed me. She told me to check under it for a bomb. Thoughtful daughter.

Tuesday

Water

I picked up Randy the next morning. We had gotten back to the social level of friend-hugs when we met at her house, polite, but playing our cards carefully. She did not want to throw in with someone she did not trust and I was scared that gold and mining might come up and God knows where that would lead, maybe to a green lefty horde from San Francisco coming down and taking over the barricades in Oaxaca.

We drove over the bay bridge and cut through the hills into the central valley and its desert heat. I closed the car windows and cranked up the air conditioning. Randy didn't say anything–this was one of our old arguments. She was for natural, I was for cool. But it was 112 degrees outside. She had changed enough to not bother fighting. We did not talk about it, though, and had a silent truce.

The freeway turned south towards LA passing through though dusty, dry brushland and then suddenly miles-long green fields, watered with networks of shiny pipes, spraying water streams up into the hot sunlight. Farm workers were everywhere in the fields, bent over and picking some vegetable, moving in a long line, shoulder to shoulder, following a conveyer belt that carried the new-cut greens to a big semi. Tents stood at the side of the fields for shade but no one was near them. I think providing shade was the new California law. But just for looks. Randy was quiet. She had worked for the farm workers when she was starting college.

"I pick my battles now," she said. "The farm workers need support, but I am spending most of my time on global warming. I didn't say anything about your driving today, but normally I would take the train over here."

I was thinking that I don't have battles now. I avoid them when I can, at least most of the time. I didn't tell her that. "I believe you are right," I said. "The world needs a lot of support."

"I spend my time helping organizations develop branded web sites and a social networking presence. I don't fight people now; I link people together."

I think I understood her. She had learned tech-speak. I only knew old-timer talk.

We pulled into Merced. East of the freeway was the rich side of town where leafy oaks, looking unnaturally cool, showed what water could do in the California central valley. On the west side of the freeway, scrub bush and weeds grew in the caked, cracked soil showing that water did not get on that side very often.

We headed due west, out on a flat, curveless road running for miles, lined for the first few blocks with fast foot drive-ins separated by liquor stores. We were heading toward Lupe.

I recognized the house from the photo on the web as we pulled in front. An air conditioner hung out the front window chugging away. The curtains were pulled tight. The place couldn't have had more than one bedroom. You could walk around it in twenty or thirty steps. I opened the car door. Heat rushed in and I broke into a sweat before I could get my foot out. Randy jumped from the car. We walked to the house.

Randy knocked. She and I stood on a small concrete porch. A green canvas awning covered it, but the sun went right through, even where there were no holes. The swinging screen door was open. Behind it, a new steel front door, the only thing new anywhere near, had double locks and looked ready to keep anyone out, or keep someone in.

I called out, *"Lupe, soy Señor Roberto, amigo de Maria en Oaxaca. Hola, hola, Lupe."*

Randy started talking gently in Spanish. I didn't know she knew the language. "We are here to help you. We are friends. We are here to help."

The door cracked open and a very young woman, looking very Oaxacan peered out. "Señor Roberto. Maria said you would come. I knew you would." The door opened and we walked in.

It was not quite so hot inside but the air conditioner rumbled and the temperature showed it was not up to the outside heat. Lupe wore a loose cotton dress and was barefoot. She stood beside a small altar–the Virgin of Oaxaca's picture was on the wall behind it and a few artificial flowers, bleached out and drooping, sat on the altar's small table. On the side was the newspaper picture of me from the assassination. Randy stopped at the picture. I walked into the room and took Lupe's hand.

"We are so happy to find you. You aunt was very worried."

Randy joined in. "I am Señor Roberto's daughter, Randy. I am happy to meet you. She hugged Lupe. Not a friendly hug, but an I-haven't-seen-you-for-years-sister kind of hug.

Lupe started crying. Randy held Lupe for a minute or two. Then she backed away, still keeping Lupe's hand tightly in hers and looking into her eyes. "Why are you here alone? Do you have enough to eat? Have you been to the doctor?"

Lupe broke out into a long story about the doctor from LA sending her to this house.

"But do you have someone to help you? Are you seeing a doctor?"

"I see the doctor. The American man across the road watches for me."

I was getting confused. I looked at Randy. She gave me another one of her incredulous looks. "Can't you see she is going to have a baby?"

Lupe was round in the stomach. I hadn't noticed. Randy and Lupe still were holding hands and talking as they sat on the two metal card chairs in the room. I couldn't follow everything, but it was about getting help and asking what Lupe wanted to do.

"We are taking Lupe away," Randy looked straight at me. She is a prisoner here with no one to help her, in this heat, with no transportation. The doctor moved her away from his house. His wife had a fit when she got back from Europe."

How did Randy learn all that so fast? I started thinking of what we could do. "Of course. We can take her back to the City and …"

"No, we will take her to a shelter and to a doctor and I have a lawyer who handles crimes like this."

I must have been looking confused. "He raped her. The doctor raped her and kept her locked in the house. That is a crime. She may be a juvenile. That is a bigger crime. We will get him."

I knew this kind of thing happened, but I was not sure what to do now. Randy was acting like this was her normal days work. Maybe it was.

"You get her things. I bet she doesn't have much. I will keep talking to her."

There were only two plastic grocery bags of clothes for me to pick up.

"Just leave everything but the clothes and her pictures. She wants her pictures," Randy yelled from the other room.

It was dark and hot in the back room. A mattress lay on the floor. A box with some of the comic book novels that you find in Mexico was in the corner. I looked in the box. Pictures were at the bottom. I threw the bags of clothes in the box and picked it up.

"Get the picture of the Virgin off the altar. She wants it. Give me the keys and we will go out to the car. It will be cooler there."

I looked in and saw Randy had given Lupe a bottle of water and was fanning her, still holding her hand. The two started out to the car. I tried to get the picture down off the wall. It was nailed through the wood frame right to the wall.

Someone yelled outside.

"What the hell are you doing here? Where are you going with her? Get away, you? Don't you kidnap that girl."

Across the street, a man standing on the porch of a house not much different than Lupe's was yelling and pointing at Randy. I stopped pulling on the frame and headed out the door. The man on the porch was big. Fat big. His arms and neck bunched into rings that looked like inflated swim toys. He stood leaning back against the wall, like he was not sure whether to come over or not.

Randy yelled back. "Lupe is going to a doctor. And butt out or I will be calling the newspapers about your doctor boss and his pregnant girlfriend and we will see how he likes you putting his name all over the news and TV."

"Hey, lady, I didn't say anything about the doctor. You leave him out of this." The fat man moved back in the shadow of the doorway watching us. He pulled out a phone.

"You leave us alone or you are in way deep shit!" Randy yelled while easing Lupe into the passenger side. Then she ran around and started the engine and car air conditioner and hopped in the back. I guess she wanted to talk to Lupe or she probably would have driven off and left me.

I got the Virgin's frame loose, stabbed myself twice with the nails sticking out the back and threw everything in the trunk. I climbed in the front seat and after looking back at Randy. We drove off throwing gravel at Lupe's front porch.

Like a miracle, the car cooled in two or three minutes.

"Randy, that was taking a chance."

"What is he going to do, shoot us? That would make a stink for his boss."

Lupe told us that the fat man brought her here from LA.

"He won't do anything. Don't worry." Randy leaned forward right next to my ear. "Lupe wouldn't have an abortion. She must have hid it from the doctor for months. Some doctor, if he can't notice that."

Randy was rubbing Lupe's shoulder speaking softly. She told her about the womans' shelter. I headed north on the freeway, Randy pointed out directions. We headed back towards San Francisco.

Randy pulled out her the cell phone and started talking away to a lawyer. I couldn't hear everything, but the doctor from LA was in big trouble.

That's when I heard the siren. Randy yelled, "keep going. They have a kidnapping alert out for us."

"Keep going, are you crazy? They will shoot us".

"Remember we have Lupe. They will chase us. They won't shoot. They don't like to kill the people they are rescuing. Our lawyer is on the way. I'll tell you when to pull over. Remember I used to handle stuff like this when we were doing demonstrations."

"Kidnapping? You handled kidnappings?"

The police car was getting closer and its loud speaker called out over and over. "Pull over immediately."

Randy tapped me on the shoulder. "Let's stop."

No disagreement from me. I slowed the car and turned out on the shoulder. One police car cut in front of us at 45 degrees; the other did the same behind us. Its speaker was really yelling then, "hold your hands where we can see them, hold your hands where we can see them."

Guns were pointing at me, lots of guns. My hands were touching the ceiling. I would have pushed right through the metal car top to help the police see my hands better if I were strong enough. One cop grabbed the door open and another grabbed me, pulled me out and pushed me hard on the ground. They grabbed all three of us and pinned the women against the car. Two cops had me lying there; they pushed my arms back and cuffed me. That is what they call it in the TV shows.

My mouth was in the dirt. The dirt was hot, hard-to-believe hot. Probably cooking-my-cheek hot. They were holding me down. I couldn't move. Then another car pulled up. Sirens. More police.

I still don't know exactly what happened. When they let me look up, the lawyer was standing there and arguing with a cop. This was after they started to arrest him.

Then they questioned Lupe in one of the police cars. The lawyer stood beside her. She pointed at me a couple times and talked about Santo Gordo and how he helped people. This did not do much for me with the cops. Finally they took us in the police cars, still in handcuffs, each of us in a different car. We went the rest of the way to Modesto. The lawyer drove behind us.

———

"How can you have a kidnapping when the victim is voluntarily going to her doctor for a pregnancy checkup?" The lawyer was yelling now at someone in charge in the police station. "Who called this dumb ass alert anyway?"

We got out pretty fast. The lawyer took us to the shelter. I sat in the back with Randy this time. Lupe rode in front. The police followed. I guess they still were not sure what was going on. I sure didn't know.

"What about my car? " I remembered it was sitting wide open on the side of the road.

They will tow it. You bought insurance didn't you? You can get the car later. Randy was not a comforting sort of person to me, like she was to Lupe. But then I was not supposed to need it. You know, being her father.

I ended up staying in a motel in Modesto. The women stayed at the shelter. The lawyer went home. I don't know about the police.

My room was just as exciting as the one back at the airport. At least I didn't see any bugs and the sheets were clean. I started my welcome-back-to-America routine—first a long hot shower, and then hopefully a nap.

But my cell phone rang while I was in the shower. I figured it was Randy.

141

"What the hell was that trick you pulled just now?" Definitely not Randy.

"We let you loose and now I am wondering why?" It was Inspector Norton from the airport.

"Why the hell were you following me?" I needed to yell at someone.

Friday

Buffet

Sometimes life is simple. Days flow into one another and time passes so softly you could be happily dead. I lived a comfortable, half-dead life in Oaxaca. I loved it. I deserved it. Come to think of it, everyone deserved it.

I was floating above it all, thinking about how relaxed I was, sitting in my room with a breeze coming in from the balcony door when the dream ended with a sharp voice in my ear.

"Chicken or Italian?"

The stewardess shook me, just so I could say no to her cold lasagna.

I forgot the soft life and woke up in a tight airplane seat smelling bad food.

My paperback had fallen into my lap. I was reading it when I fell asleep, a mystery, a little too bloody for me, but one I knew it would wrap up every loose end. That was what I liked–knots tied, ends nicely trimmed and everything concluded neatly. Not like real life.

I was flying back to Oaxaca. Lupe sat beside me, scared of airplanes and holding my hand. Randy was still in the States, working on the L.A. doctor. He was scared for his reputation, she said. The thing had become legally messy: "consensual" he said; "he was the boss," Lupe said.

Inspector Norton did not get his narco-connection by following me–maybe he still was–but he had stopped yelling on the phone, threatening to bring me in.

I had a call the day before from my friend Arturo. He wanted to know what was going on. "There are rumors about you that are not good," he told me.

Efraím sent me a cryptic email that ended: "Sometimes power lures you in and squeezes softly; sometimes it just bites. Be careful." He was getting philosophical. Or reading fortune cookies.

Lupe sat beside me, illegal as hell, but going the wrong way–to Mexico not to the States like the normal ones. She had a passport that Randy borrowed from a friend. It looked like Lupe, and said she was from Oaxaca, just had a different name. Weird, but Randy said she knew about this sort of thing, just trust me. And according to Randy, Lupe needed to be back home a lot more than in court fighting the doctor. Randy said I needed to take her there. If we got caught, we both would go for another interrogation. But I was getting good at them.

Señora Concepción would be waiting at the airport, probably with a band and a couple priests to celebrate our return and plan the unborn baby's life.

144

We landed and got thru immigration and customs and everything else. We saw faces outside the glass. They were all at the door: Maria, the Señora, her son Jorge and his wife, the kids, the Directora from the newly painted preschool, a couple neighbors, the priest, Efraím, Arturo, everyone, my whole Oaxaca family.

They made a hug and handshake line at the airport entrance stretching from the door all the way out to the sidewalk. The Señora was first and her driver last in line, with everyone else spread out in between. Lupe and I hugged them all.

When I got to Arturo, I spoke quietly. It didn't make much difference with all the noise, but I wanted this private. "Can I come to your house and explain. This has gotten messy. You said it would go away, but I am afraid it is here to stay."

"I know. I heard about the gold mine. Come tonight."

I had a similar talk with Efraím. Tonight was catch-up time. I just hoped no one else, like Señor Ruiz or Inspector Norton, wanted to join in.

But the afternoon return of Lupe was much too happy an event for us not to have a fiesta and forget everything else, like gold, dead fish, and bodies.

We took over the airport exit area and shooed the guards away. Well, maybe it was the Señora that did that. After ten minutes of her thanking God and blessing the returning Oaxacans, me included, Maria, Lupe and the Señora climbed into a van that she had commandeered from one of her connections. She announced, "Today is a special day. We are having lunch at the Hacienda to celebrate."

Arturo and Efraím waved as they walked away, going back to work. Most everyone else took this as a great excuse for an afternoon off.

No objection from me there.

We drove fifteen minutes with me sitting in the van's wonderfully large front seat, untangling airplane-dead legs, listening to the happy gabble in the back. We pulled into the restaurant parking lot and reassembled at a long table. No one reserved anything there. You just showed up and there was always another table, somewhere. The restaurant was spread out over a couple acres of real grass lawn, not so common down here, a scrubby version of grass that barely covered the ground but made it cooler. We sat outside on benches and plastic chairs pulled up to tables shaded with umbrellas. The restaurant's grand attraction was its playground. Besides the normal swings and slides, a World War II propeller passenger plane, retired from the local airline a couple years ago, sat looking ready to take off and, beside it, a full scale, replica pirate ship was pulling into its concrete port. The place was crawling with kids who climbed anything they could grab, the cockpit, the rigging, even the wings and motors.

The food maybe wasn't the best, but there was a lot of it. That was fine with me after the long trip. They served a buffet with everything Mexican lined up simmering in two-foot wide, painted clay bowls. A charcoal grill about the size of a Chevrolet was roasting lamb and goat and beef in the back. To finish you off, a mountain of desserts, most too sticky and too sweet, were piled in a corner next to the DJ and his speakers.

Even on a workday the restaurant was busy. There were always birthdays and Saint Days and God-knows-what days for families to celebrate. This was the place for families: big ones of ten, twenty, or thirty people, but everyone under twelve immediately ran to the plane and pirate ship. The adults took samples from a waitress who carried a tray of thimble-sized plastic cups filled with pink and yellow and amber mezcal. Some were real mezcal and burned; the rest were fruity *cremas* that had a mezcal base covered with a sweet fruit cream that you could drink all day and then be carried home. Your pick. I took both. And then a real shot glass or two.

Señora Concepción loved this place. She could rule over her table and make pronouncements and promote or relegate to the second table anyone in her retinue. Today I sat on her right, Lupe on the left and Maria next to Lupe.

"We are here to give thanks to God and to Señor Roberto." I was keeping good company in her eyes after the rescue. "And to tell you the wonderful news that Lupe will be having a baby boy. We shall call him Beto, our new little Roberto."

"Big Beto," she looked at me and smiled the biggest one she had ever done in front of me, "and little Beto."

She did not need to check with the mother on this. That was the old Mexican way, the older woman ran the house. And it was why Efraím was not living near his mother. And Arturo wanted to. Families are complicated. The Señora has told me God wanted it that way.

I could not really complain, but I wished that the Señora had explained the parentage of the little one a bit better to the assembled friends. As she kept looking back and forth from Lupe to me, I was beginning to feel that maybe this Mexican family thing was going too far. Then the Señora added, "His Tío, Uncle Roberto brought Lupe and the baby back." She did not have to mention from where, it was always the evil el Norte in her mind, the place that ate the young men and women of her Oaxaca. "I have been praying every day and every night and had two masses in the church and today God answered my prayers."

She hugged me and she hugged Lupe and I was getting scared about the next move, maybe she would push me over to Lupe, but I was determined to stay a Tío and not start being a Papi Roberto, no matter what the Señora did.

It ended, thank God. I went to the apartment and got indigestion from Mexican food for the first time in years. And this was before Efraím arrived

His honking woke me from my siesta. Short regular blasts. Then a minute silence. Then honking again. Efraím did not like to leave his cab during business hours. I got up, walked to the window and waved at him to stop. "Enough, *basta, basta.*" I grabbed my hat and jacket and ran out.

A big afternoon storm was passing through. Raindrops about an inch across were battering the street. Everyone walked quickly, head down. You could drown by looking up too long. The storm would drift over to another valley in fifteen minutes, but just then Oaxaca was soaked and the puddles were two feet across. I held the jacket over my head, jumped the gutter now running like a river and climbed into the cab.

"Hola, amigo. Let's take a drive." Efraím had his lucky Cruz Azul jacket on. He only wore that to soccer matches or when he needed a special help. He said he dunked it in holy water once. That was the last time it was washed. Something was up.

"What's happened up on the you-know-what, where the things I like to eat with fins live in the water?" I was trying for silence but this was the best I could do.

"Don't worry, our golden silence is over. Now is the time to talk. You need to tell me everything, like I am your priest. I need to figure out what is going on and you probably know something important."

I wanted to tell him anyway. I needed to talk, but Efraím kept going, "so far, I have heard nothing about the trout murder—that's strange. I have my ears out everywhere and no one knows anything."

His ears were cab drivers all over the city. I think I was one of his ears too, listening to the expats and telling him about them. I wondered who his other ears might be.

"Something big is going to happen. We need to figure it out."

I was not sure why I needed to figure this out, after all the warnings to lay low that he had given me in the past. Efraím had his finger in lots of things. This was affecting him in some way. He did not stop thinking about his cab unless there was a personal reason.

"But you said to stay out of this stuff."

"I know, but living twenty years in el Norte makes you strange. I started getting curious. Like one of your nosy *reporteros*."

Efraím was only nosy when something mattered to him. Otherwise he waited until the news drifted his way.

"Where is this gold mine of Señor Ruiz? Is it near the old mine on the hill by the trout restaurant?"

I remembered it was somewhere down south. I had written down the coordinates after that day of writing about the gold mine report. I never looked exactly where it was.

Efraím waited while I squeezed out the car, ran back in the rain, got soaked in five steps because I forgot my jacket, fumbled for my key and got wetter. Finally I got inside and looked on my computer. I printed out a map and hurried back. The place was somewhere on the other side of Ocotlán, a town about an hour or so away.

Efraím looked at the map and got as excited as I had ever seen him. "You are hiring me at a very special tourist rate tomorrow. You buy gas, I buy beer. And we will go look at this gold mine. Maybe have lunch. I know a place that specializes in *birria de chivo*. *Estilo Jalisco*."

"Goat stew from Jalisco? For that I am ready."

"Fun, food and frijoles for you tomorrow, Mr. Santo. And another day of cab driver work for me."

We did not talk about what happened last time we went out for a long ride, out to the Trout Farm with its little dead fish and big dead Mexican.

Everyone around me was trying to figure out what was going on. First Randy with the doctor in the rescue and now Efraím looking for gold. And it looked like I was going along as number two, the sidekick. That's bad because sidekicks are expendable. Like old horses, broken wagons and the wrappers on your hot dogs. They all can be tossed. I would have to keep an eye out. TV taught me that. I watched westerns too, not just detective shows.

"That's it. Time is up in the cab." Efraím, the new business-like Efraím, had finished.

"Hey, you aren't done talking, are you?" I wanted to know more.

"That's it. The Americanos taught me to go straight to the point. None of the 'would you be so kind, sir' stuff, except for paying customers."

"Hey, I'll pay you. I want to hire you right now."

"Surely, Señor. Would you be so kind as to give me your destination and we will be on our way."

"Let's head over to Arturo's."

"That water guy, right?"

I had kept my two friends apart. They lived in different worlds, but maybe it was time to introduce them. "He is the water guy. Maybe you two should meet."

"Not this afternoon. Got to make some money. I'm not a tourist here, you forget that sometimes."

We got to Arturo's as he was arriving from work. Efraím said goodbye and drove off in his normal cloud of smoke. Arturo welcomed me back. His wife Carmen came out and welcomed me back. And then, last out of the house, their daughter, Victoria, welcomed me too. It felt good to be here.

The females cleared out soon to leave Arturo and me alone. Carmen suddenly had to go out shopping and Victoria had an appointment for class over at the church. The priest there was preparing her and some other young impressionables from the barrio for first communion. They had to learn what a sin was and what it wasn't. We older folks knew. We had tried them both. Maybe one more than the other.

"Oh my friend, what a life you lead. I have heard rumors about you and Señor Ruiz. We must talk." Arturo pulled me into the house and handed me a beer. He took one too and we sat at his kitchen table. The calendar on the wall had a picture of the new Governor smiling down on us. When you work for the state you have to be careful.

"I need to explain life to you a little," Arturo said. "Ruiz would never tell you where his gold mine is located."

Wait a minute. I did not tell Arturo about the mine. How did he know? I forgot he seemed to know everything that was going on. I guess he had his network too, like the Señora, but one inside the government.

With this news, I started thinking maybe the trip tomorrow with Efraím would be a joyride, with nothing at the end but a nice view, no gold. That was OK with me. The last ride to the Trout Farm was not so joyful.

"Or …," Arturo started down another path of thought, "Señor Ruiz might be trying to sabotage someone else´s gold mine. Like for instance if the ex-Governor had rights to a gold mine, Ruiz might want to sabotage it, spread stories about it, give out secrets. Especially to someone who had links in the eco-activist network up north. That's what they say about you."

I guess everyone knows my history now. I might as well write a book to save them some time figuring me out. But there might be gold at the end of my trip tomorrow in the taxi, just it is not Ruiz' gold. Then it won't be only a joy ride. But, I hope, a ride with nothing too dead on the far end.

Arturo took me to the computer and showed me something he had found, something I had not seen for years. He had been doing more detective work than me. Maybe the same snooping on me as Ruiz. I downgraded my detective rating a couple notches. The screen listed news clippings about me on the web. He clicked one from many years back. In the picture above the article, Randy–she was Rhonda then–carried a sign 'Stop the Machine' painted over a big skull and crossbones. Behind her a hundred or so people were standing, mostly teenagers and kids raising their fists. The headline read, "Protests Against Local Mine."

I read the story. Randy was identified as the daughter of a mine official, Robert Evans. The web kept no secrets.

"Your daughter is still an *activista*?" He looked intently at me.

"Yes, maybe even more, now."

"She sounds like a good person. Like the activists down her. Just here they have to be very careful." Arturo was smiling at me. I started to explain my relationship with my daughter, but realized it was much too complicated for a quick explanation and I did not understand it anyway.

Arturo quit smiling and took a deep breath. "Maybe Ruiz thinks you will tell your daughter and all the activist people about the mine, where it is, and about the development plan. It might have been a plan that the ex-Governor and his dinosaurs were working on. A plan that Ruiz stole. This could be a way for Ruiz to stick a knife in the ex-Governor and his dinosaur friends."

Arturo kept going. He continued to set me straight on his theory. "Protests would come to the ex-Governor´s mine. Reporters would come. The World Bank would come. It would cost the ex-Governor time, which he does not have. It would cost him money, which he does have, but does not want to share. Ruiz may be using you as a pipeline, not a mine expert. You need to be careful. Remember life is complicated."

Friday

Corn on the Cob, Fried Bananas

Boom. ShhhhhhhhhhhhKaBOOM.

Fireworks. Another holiday. I thought about it a minute and remembered. This was the big one, the night Virgin Mary does her blastoff from earth and goes up to heaven. It was Assumption of the Virgin night.

I had taken a cab back from Arturo´s. It was about nine and finally pretty dark. The cab was trapped in a long line of cars sitting still, not honking, just idling and waiting. Efraím was not driving this time; he would have bypassed all this. The traffic jam had given me time to think a lot about what Arturo had said and what I would tell Efraím. Probably everything.

A procession from the local church had taken over the street and held the cars captive. In front of me, Virgin Mary was all in blue, life-sized, and covered with fine gauze billowing like an outsized wedding veil. She stood on a platform carried by ten men. They were straining with the load. They moved in unison, all wearing neatly pressed, but old, well-worn suits and ties. Ahead of the Virgin, a small band, lead by a tuba and bass drum, headed into new improvisations on some hymn, guiding the Virgin forward. In the very front, before the band, two *coheteros*—I don't even know if we have a word in English anymore after OSHA made things safe for us—two fireworks men lit a rocket about every twenty feet as the procession moved ahead. And in the rear, walking slowly behind the Virgin, a hundred or so followers, mostly women wrapped in dark shawls, sang loudly, carried candles and looked at peace with the world, not noticing the explosions over their heads and the church bells ringing non-stop.

The cab inched along behind the procession. I paid and got out to walk. I was only a couple blocks from my place anyway.

The procession reached the church and headed in through its tall stone doorway. I stood watching for a minute as the Virgin was placed in her normal home, next to the altar. She smiled down and was the only one who didn't jump when the next fireworks barrage went off.

"Roberto, *Hola*."

I turned and there were Carlos, Lance, Francesca—the expat gang.

"You're back. Here for the Assumption?"

They did not ask where I had gone. That was good. They were watching the procession. Tourists love to watch these religious things. Expats wait for the big ones when hundreds of people, some praying, some watching, come alive on the streets of their neighborhoods. This is not the rehearsed, TV-based spectacle that we get fed up north. Here you feel like God came down, abandoned the internet and airwaves for some rocket smoke and, maybe, a couple ground-shaking miracles too.

"Of course, I came to watch," I lied. "Who would miss this?"

It was good to see all their faces, now looking up at a four-story fireworks display about twenty feet from the church door. The townspeople put these things up in a day or so, tying together bamboo and sticks to make a frame for the fireworks, building the *castillo*, the Virgin's short-lived, exploding castle.

Carlos was chewing at some corn on the cob he got on the corner. Lark was dealing with her order of steamed bananas from the cart in front of the church. Both treats normally were covered with mayonnaise and chilies in Mexico, but we gringos leave that off, ferociously halting vendors when they move to slather it on. Mayo down here, like the Mexican people, loves the sun. Open gallon jars sit out for weeks. Believing Catholics not only survive it but take it like a sacrament; we Protestants are afraid to try. We have no to faith to guide us in our eating.

I gave everyone a big Mexican hug and Carlos offered me a shot of mezcal. I took it and decided to stay. It was time for the big show to start.

Two young Mexican men approached and stood by me at the church door. They were the first of the night's *toritos*, little bulls, and they would begin the fireworks show. They held large paper maché cones, about three feet tall over their heads. The cones were covered with rockets and roman candles and all the other types of fireworks my parents never let me try as a kid. They were not the safe-and-sane ones we had up north. I did not know their names, only that a lot of black powder was about five feet away from me and a *cohetero* was lighting it.

The *toritos* stood still until the fuses sizzled. Then they took off in a wild spinning two-step. The band joined in with something four-four and danceable. A second later the first explosion rocked us, and we were sprayed with sparks from roman candles mounted just over the *torito's* head. A spinner screamed like the bombs falling in old war movies and ended with an explosion that dwarfed the cherry bombs guys set off in bathrooms back when I was in high school. And all this blew up on the top of the *torito's* cone-covered head.

The two young men danced in circles and swung the exploding cones in big, high arcs, all in time with the music.

Once when he had finished his dancing, I asked a young *torito*, "don't you get burned?"

"Of course," he answered looking as though I were the world's stupidest gringo. This was a macho show. Young men lined up to dance, young bulls going at it, doing their best before the Virgin to show themselves off. As though she might pick one for some special errand. Maybe she would. This was Mexico and that sort of thing had happened before.

The *cahetero* brought out two more of the large, explosive paper cones and two more young men came forward to dance. These were more daring. They chased young women and even older ones back into doorways. Small boys came out from the crowd and taunted the *toritos*, running behind until the fireworks got turned on them, with sparks showering their backs as they ducked and ran. They screamed, partly joy and partly fear, as they took off, some back to their mothers.

We expats stood near the church entrance along with older parishioners and had something of a refuge from the *toritos*. They looked our way, but always veered off before getting too close to the door.

We were breathless during the first pair's dancing, but by the time ten had their turn and an hour had passed, we were talking and eating again and only twitched a little when the explosions shook us.

As the last pair finished dancing, the tall fireworks tower, the Virgin´s *castillo*, started going off. It was built in levels. The bottom started exploding first. Spinning wheels, each maybe six feet across and powered by roman candles, lit the churchyard a cherry color. In four or five minutes they sputtered out and the crowd crept forward, closer to the *Castillo*, waiting for the next part of the show. The front edge of onlookers was up to about fifteen feet from the explosions. People were bunched together, going back across the street and down to the corner. We gringos stayed in the church doorway, so we could duck in if things went wrong. That happened once or twice a year in Mexico. But the crowd had faith in the Virgin who was ready to head up to heaven. They could hide under her cape. Or maybe someplace else, like up in heaven with her if the explosions did them in.

We expats had no heavenly faith. We believed in solid stone, like the doorway. It would protect us down here on earth. We would never make good Catholics.

The next layer of the fireworks tower had more spinning wheels. Different colors, smaller but more frequent explosions. Then as these died down the twenty foot tall Virgin revealed herself standing high over our heads with red and blue flares outlining her form. Her pyrotechnics lit the night for a while as a shower of blue sparks shot down, cascading over her outline, forming another of this lady's veils. And then to show us how she went to heaven, a spinning circle of jets, her halo five feet across, shot up in the air. It rose like a flying saucer or maybe the Virgin's soul, or maybe just a rocket-powered Frisbee, soaring over our heads. It was still spinning and climbing as it lifted over the church.

The band banged away fighting the fireworks for attention. The tuba solos grew less connected to the melodies and the drummers forgot the four-four beat and discovered ancient rhythms that were noisy and indecipherable to us gringos.

The final layer in the tower at the very top, celebrating the Virgins liftoff, lit up with more spinning, more colors.

Then, behind the Castillo, on the concrete walkway, mortars exploded, letting us know they were the real thing by shaking even the stone wall, firing bowling-ball sized bombs, full of heavy explosives, high in the air, two or three hundred feet up, and making huge showers of sparks and fiery blossoms in the night. They were the fireworks we see on July 4th and New Years in the States. Only these mortars were not firing from some barge anchored a half mile out from the shore. They were just behind the tower, 50 feet away. No fences held us back. Just another one of the plastic crime-scene tapes wrapped from tree to tree and then around two chairs near the church door.

A final barrage ended it all. The Virgin made it into heaven and we were all deaf. Carlos yelled for us to go across the street pointing at the Café Picho sign. It was empty when we got there. Most families were heading home. The show was over. The church door was closing.

We gringos took a big table in the front. We had to shout to get past the ringing in our ears at first and slapped each other on the back, and smiled. We looked like we had just seen the second coming. It was great. Religion works best when it is full of explosions to make you deaf and has lots of bright lights to blind you.

A few minutes later, we could hear again and started more normal levels of conversation. I forgot Arturo and Efraím for a while with these people. It was a gringo family party, with all of us happy to see each other, saying nothing serious, just a little froth before the hard work on beer and chips. We kept up the smiles but our conversations fizzled about two beers down, so we just ate and smiled again.

I liked these displaced folks, maybe loved them in my way, but we had neither the courtesies of the Mexicans to keep a conversation going or the deep links of blood to give you a thousand shared events and characters to pull out for dissection. We had politics–complaints about Mexico and about Bush. They wore us down fast. We had the weather. It was good. We had our medical complaints, but people only wanted to talk about their own. And we had our little group to gossip about.

For any other topic, I could not get past the holding back I had learned growing up. Maybe women could do it. But not us old gringo men. We men just knew how to mock, sometimes gently, sometimes harshly. Like we did back in high school. We could talk, but not about anything that mattered.

We expats, retired and cut loose from caring, seemed to return to a quasi-teenaged existence, but this time nothing hurt too much or pained us badly or, even worse, felt very good like it did back in the high school hallways and gyms, growing up.

Some of us tried to get the old inner fires burning again, being part of the life around us. We worried about poor kids and taught them English. But kids came and went and became interchangeable. We worried about poverty, but never really felt it. We gave a little to charity or, at least, to some small young woman, really a child, nursing her infant on the sidewalk, holding out her hand, or maybe to an older beggar looking her practiced piteousness in front of some church.

Or worse we chased after someone way too young. But that always turned out bad.

162

Our fires were out. We gringos were shells of people down here. We had not brought our families and our families' futures with us. Just us, floating on the surface of Mexico, unable to dive into its life. That was our expat life after heading south.

We were not like the Mexican immigrants up north who had to fight hard to survive. Their fires had to stay lit. Maybe we needed it tougher down here.

We avoided life. Just watched. Some with their eyes only half open. Some drank too much. Some smoked too much dope. Pain reduction was the order of the day for many. No deep feelings and not even much action.

I liked these people though; they were good, but only half alive. Their other halves were still in the States, having babies and jobs and living on as children and grandchildren, or maybe just as old friends while we took the sun down in Mexico.

Then again, life up north would have been the same for many of us. Our kids had grown and left. Marriages had failed. Work had ended and connections died. There were no town squares up north with benches everywhere like here, and it was too cold or too hot outside anyway, so we would have sat in our rooms. It was better down here–sitting in the parks watching life running around, not watching TV. Watching the living, not watching thirty-minute chunks of some Hollywood fantasy.

We finished our beer and guacamole, hugged quietly and went home. Mostly by ourselves. Maybe with a book. Maybe with a bottle or a smoke. Making sure that life was simple.

I was only a little different from the others gringos. They didn't worry about assassins or murders or gold mines. I did. Fear wakes you up.

I got back to my place. I saw the Señora´s family up on the rooftop terrace. There were about a dozen, counting Maria and Lupe. Cousins must have come in from the pueblos. They were watching fireworks. Señora Concepción waved for me to come join her and the family.

Oaxaca's main show started down by the cathedral. I know the one at our church sounded big, but we only had the mortars going for five minutes. Down at the cathedral, there could have been a war and it would not have sounded any different.

Maria and Lupe walked toward me.

"Randy called a little while ago," Lupe smiled at me as she spoke. "She asked me to say hello to you."

"What else did she say?"

"She just wanted to see if the baby and I were OK. We talked mostly about the baby kicking. She approved of the name."

Everyone seemed to approve except me. I guess we will be big Beto and little Beto. I should get used to it.

"Any message for me? "

"Just hello." You would think she had something more to say than that. But, then, I didn't call her. Maybe tomorrow.

Maria came over and hugged me again. I was starting to feel passed around. I decided to call it quits before the final bang of the night´s fireworks.

"Goodnight, Señora. I must go rest. I am going for a trip in the mountains early tomorrow."

Damn, I should be quiet. Now she will want to know where and what and why. "Sorry, but I am very tired, goodnight."

Saturday

Birria

I got up early, filled my water bottle, grabbed my sun screen and mosquito repellant, and put on my walking shoes. I was ready and waiting in my room.

The house was noisy. Señora Concepcíon was talking with a neighbor. Maria was mopping downstairs. The bleach smell came up to my room, not too strong, but enough to remind you that battles against dirt were more fierce down here where the spiders, cockroaches, and microbes grew faster than in the north. They used chemical weapons that we had abandoned long ago for things like scrubby bubbles and tidy bowls.

The children were leaving for school, yelling at each other about who moved their *mochilas*, their backpacks. One was a Sponge Bob and the other a Dora. The *conquista* was still going on, especially for the young ones. They knew the latest US styles better than I ever would.

The Señora's son and his wife were leaving too, he to an office job and she to a clinic. She was a nurse. I saw her working sometimes in the evening. People stopped by the house to get a shot, bringing their syringes and vials with them. Most people had someone in the family do it, because it cost money, about 60 cents, for a nurse to stick the needle in. But the Señora's daughter was known for giving pain-free injections. They used big cheap needles here, some reused many times, probably a little rusty and not so sharp; so doing it painlessly was important for a nurse´s reputation.

Injections and pain were big down here. Sticking yourself was not much different from wrapping thorns around your neck during Easter week. It hurt. A little suffering always made you better. A nurse was like a priest, leading you through pain to the promised land of health or maybe heaven.

I was not hurting much today. Just the normal aches before my caffeine. But I was waiting to have my first coffee with Efraím after we took off on our gold hunt, so I was not my happy morning self.

Of course, he was late–some business about getting his wife's cousin to the bus station. She had shown up at his house last night, unannounced–normal for relatives in Oaxaca–ready for a bus trip to the coast. All went well. Efraím dropped her off and was only a half hour late.

We stopped at a yet another new espresso stand on the way out of town. He stayed in the cab and I ran in and ordered our drinks to go. Soon even the street vendors will be selling espresso at traffic lights, along with peeled fruits, sodas and windshield wipers.

We drove south. It was a good morning for a ride. The clouds shielded us from the hottest rays of the sun, the cab was cooled by the wind rushing in, and we had the car stereo singing old Mexican ballads about heroes and villains. I held my second espresso grande in my hand and sang along.

It was easy to forget everything from the past weeks looking out at the mountains, watching the clouds snagged on their summits. Blue sky showed through, like veins in the whiteness and, sometimes, like large pools above the slow but constantly churning currents pushing the clouds back and forth in the sky. These clouds had been lifted up the mountains as the winds blew in from the coast. Most of their water fell on the lower slopes making it a wet jungle down there. As the clouds climbed inland to the Oaxaca valley, they grew whiter and drier. Some water made it here almost every day this time of year and we got short, heavy showers like the one yesterday. On some days water from the Atlantic fell, on some days it came from the Pacific. Winds swirled back and forth. Oaxaca was a mixing bowl half way between two oceans. Its skies were always changing. You never knew what was next. You just knew it was coming.

Efraím was quiet on this trip. I got none of his historical references explaining the current mess in Mexico and the world. He just looked ahead and drove. I looked out the window. We climbed over the hills, now green after the late summer´s afternoon rains, towards another valley. Dirt roads lead off to small clusters of one story, flat-roofed sun brick houses. They sat in the fields on the hillsides, each with rows of some crop, probably corn, half grown–I don't know much about plants. Most houses were plastered over and painted, some in pinks, some yellows and blues, but many in a cheaper white. Poorer families never finished the first floor and had bare bricks and sheets of corrugated metal leaning against the wall to hold out the wind and water. Sometimes there were thatched roofs, but usually those were just for roadside stands selling what they called real Oaxacan foods.

I saw a burro. Not so many were here as when I first arrived ten years ago. This was pickup country now. Not big pickups, the F150s were for big shots. Little Japanese pickups, the kind we had in the States in the 70s, they were the ones for country people. Whole families crowded into the front seat until the kids were old enough to hold on and then they stood in the back. Sometimes with a goat or an unsteady cow riding next to them. No seat belts here.

Sometimes the trucks were so overloaded that their tires looked flat. Cement, sand, and stones got piled high on these trucks that veered through curves on their way to add another wall or maybe a cement roof over one of the houses in the hills.

The road was straight after we passed into the next valley. We slowed slightly as we came to the outer edges of Ocotlán, the next town, and passed the normal mix of roadside food stops, car repair shops and used tire stands. The repair shops had lean-to roofs and sometimes a tarp covering the transmissions and engines lying on the ground, their pistons and camshafts showing, probably waiting for parts to be scavenged from some other car. Men and boys, the sons learning the trade, with grease covered hands and sometimes faces, lay under the cars working or sat around with the older ones smoking. Rows of used tires were for sale too. Some that I would call usable, but all were usable down here. This was a true recycling nation with most too poor to buy new. They got hand-me-downs from the next step up, the city workers, and drove them to the last strand of reinforced wire buried deep in the rubber, the ones that we gringos never see.

Not everyone was poor. Every once and a while, a BMW or Mercedes powered by us, dark windows closed, speeding ahead of everything. And there were buses and piggy-back semis, loaded with oil and chemicals, and sometimes a smaller flatbed truckload of American goods bought at the Walmart or big town market back in Oaxaca, heading to stock a family-run general store in a village up in the mountains.

Ocotlán sneaks up on you. First a couple small stores looked lost at the edge of fields. Then evenly spaced jacaranda trees lined the road, more plastic bags were caught in the bushes on the roadside and speed bumps came every quarter mile. You saw clusters of stores and a couple of the funny, three-wheeled taxis. Then, suddenly you were at a neat town square with its bandshell, a big market on one side and, of course, the stone church across the street.

We didn't have time to look closely at any of this today. Efraím barely moved his eyes from the road as we started the opposite journey, leaving town and watching the buildings getting farther apart. In ten minutes we were back to open countryside. Then we started slowing when one of the big PEMEX gas stations got closer.

"We are stopping to fill up."

Efraím had finally spoken. I was tempted to give him a hard time about his new found silence, but he did not look in the mood. I got out and went to pay.

"About another hour." Efraím started the engine and concentrated again on the road. I resumed my joyride.

We passed a series of half-buried truck tires, big ones, taller than me, with ads hand painted in drippy white paint on the sides. They announced some little restaurant coming up soon. The tires reminded me of the countryside leaving Baltimore, not the countryside now, but the one I saw on road trips when I was a kid. Those trips were my first joyrides with me sitting in the front seat playing with maps. We stopped at places advertised on the tires. No chain restaurants were around then, only family stops, where the family lived in the back of the restaurant and got up early to start cooking and stayed up late to clean. There were homemade candy stores pushing peanut logs, along with barbecue joints that had 55 gallon drums, sliced in half and smoking away. Some had chicken wire zoos full of alligators and snakes behind the restaurants when we went into the South. All had messages painted on tires out on the highway. Just like here. I had forgotten.

Mexico kept drawing me back to a world that had disappeared in my country. A world where families controlled the side roads. Now, those were gone in the US.

And they were going fast here. Big companies were moving in all the time.

We climbed into the mountains, leaving the influence of el Norte, even the influence of the Spanish, who left behind their church and their genes after they had taken most of the gold and silver. Villages were farther from the road. You could see them high up in the hills. We passed ruins of pyramids, still unexcavated by city archeologists. We passed men in handmade clothes, wearing straw hats that they had woven themselves, working in smaller and smaller fields, tending crops and leading animals.

I was gazing out the side window, fading a bit, when Efraím spoke again. "My friend, I must confess. I did not tell you everything. The man who died, the man we saw, I found out yesterday, he was from my village. That is where we are going."

"But we are going to the coordinates that Señor Ruiz gave me."

"Precisely, that is where my village is located."

Efraím was the one who told me God arranges coincidences. It makes God seem like a bad mystery writer trying to make things fit in a story without enough characters. But God is mysterious. I believe that. I never know why things happen. Like why he was messing around near the Trout Farm. And why was Efraím leading me up in the mountains again.

"We will go to the gold mine, the one listed in your coordinates, but first I must stop by my village, and pay respects."

We turned on a dirt road. A highway sign gave the name of the village, "Santa Maria" for the first part, like most small pueblos down here, and ending with one of those ancient unpronounceable Indian names that had lots of q´s and x´s in it.

The taxi bounced along for a mile or so. We were climbing. I hoped no one was coming down because there was only one lane, with a long drop over one side and a sheer wall on the other. Someone would have to back up if we met. Efraím honked every time we approached a curve. No one ever honked back. Then I saw why.

The road was blocked. An old VW sat in the middle of the road facing sideways. Two men with rifles leaned against it. The rifles looked like the ones that guerillas used in war movies a long time ago. One man wore the white cotton pants and loose shirt of the villagers; the other, jeans and a tee shirt. Both wore the small Oaxacan sombreros that looked like children's hats to me, but all the pueblo men here wore them. They were not afraid of the sun like us gringos.

Efraím waved and yelled. He got out and told me to stay inside. He talked a while and then pointed back at me. I was wondering how he explained me.

"I had to tell him that you were Santo Gordo. Someone might recognize you and think you worked for the government so we have to explain things. You are tied in with the government after that picture in the paper. I told him you were OK, but watch out. They will want to make sure. Now we go pay respects."

I had not been counting on this.

The men rolled the VW back into a niche in the mountain on the side of the road. We drove past. No friendly waves. Just stares.

Suddenly the road was paved and led to a new concrete bridge crossing a deep river, running fast with water, the result of all the afternoon rains. Efraím's pueblo was on the other side. A couple paved streets, a couple dirt ones, a church, a school and dozens of houses laid out like a cross on the hillside.

"That is my father's house." He pointed at a house near the school. "My house is the yellow one up on the hill." Efraím pointed to a small rise behind the pueblo. That's three years savings in the States. It is my special retirement plan when my taxi dies and I move back here, out of the city."

"*Que bonito*! What a beautiful place." I was surprised at how well maintained everything looked.

"Everyone sends money from the States to build a house. Some cousin lives there and takes care of it until you return. Some never return, but everyone tries to come back for Christmas. The pueblo is lucky that some of its men have done well up north. A couple have their own gardening companies. One, a restaurant. They paid for the bridge and the roads. The pueblo sends out a tax notice to the ones who left. You want to come back when you are old, you pay. You pay anyway because it is your pueblo. I bought both the tubas in the official band."

I bet he had given a lot more than that.

We parked on the main street. One of the houses had a black bow hung over the door.

"That is it. We go in. You be quiet, nod when I say something and pray in front of the body, like I do."

That's what we did. We walked past the men sitting in white plastic lawn chairs on one side and the women sitting on a bench on the other. The women were talking; the men silent. The body lay in a wooden coffin surrounded by marigolds. The dead guy looked up towards the sky, like he was waiting for something to happen.

I walked up and prayed, like Efraím, mumbling away for a minute or so. Then we sat with the men. A woman brought us a coke with a straw in it. We sat silently. Mezcal was passed. We drank. Everyone was tense.

Everyone but the children, that is. They were running, yelling, playing some kind of tag. Two boys walked up to the coffin. I think the older one was showing his brother what dead is. The younger one, standing on his toes, touched the cheek of the body. Then ran away. No one stopped them. Death happened here and you saw it. It was good to learn young.

Efraím walked up to a group of men who looked like they were in charge. They did the Mexican hug. One of the older men must have been his father. But there was no time for introductions today. They stood off in a corner and talked. I sat near the body and thought about the dead guy. I guess he was the one I saw up by the Trout Farm. Dead men look a lot alike.

Efraím came back and nodded for me to follow. We went past the body again. Another quick prayer and then to his cab.

"What was he doing at the Trout Farm? Why was he killed?" It seemed like time for Efraím to tell me what was going on.

"I will explain later. Let's just see what is here for now."

It was all confused to me. It looked like it was going to stay that way for a while.

"They said we can go to the site. They blocked company trucks and cars that come here for the survey. The company was drilling samples last month."

"It is a mine site. Ruiz did not lie to me."

"Of course he lied. We just do not know what part was a lie." Efraím seemed sure about this. I did not have time to talk about what Arturo had told me, about Ruiz using me to let the activists in the States know what was happening.

We drove to the edge of the concrete road, about a quarter mile, and then started on a rough road that had more big rocks and holes than anything else. Efraím maneuvered the cab so that we only scraped a couple times. At least the road was flat. No more cliffs and long drops to the valley. We were crossing a smooth rock surface, something that had welled up millions of year ago, I bet, from a volcano or earthquake and left a strange outer space surface. Then we crossed a stream. Water was up to the car´s doorway. Efraím trusted the cab more than I did. I was thinking about the long walk back to the pueblo if the cab broke down.

Then I saw it. A drilling rig sat by itself on the rock. It was still. No one was around.

"The pueblo men chased away everyone from the mining company. The townspeople expect the army to come with the mining company men when they return to reopen the site."

"The army?"

"Who did you think? Some negotiating committee." Efraím looked determined. I had never seen him this way before.

"What can we do?" I was pretty sure I couldn't do much. But I was wondering about the village. I had heard rumors about villages that just disappeared when the army got involved.

"We go back. The pueblo has friends in the court and in the government. They will work on their friends. And keep their guns ready."

Then I heard the thump. It was not loud. It hit the back door on my side. Efraím threw the car into reverse and we started setting records for driving backwards.

"Keep your head down." Efraím yelled over the whine of the transmission. It was not made for going backwards at this speed.

The only place to put my head down was between my knees and they took up all the room, so I slouched as much as I could.

We crossed the river. Fast this time. Water splashed in the window.

Efraím looped the car into a half circle and stopped abruptly. We started frontwards throwing rocks in the air, sending a cloud of dust back towards the mine. We were going way too fast for the road, if you want to call it that, and I was bouncing and hitting my head when we did the big bounces.

"What happened?" I was trying to figure out what was going on.

"They shot my taxi, my only taxi." I thought it was a rock flying up. But it was a bigger whump than the rocks. I was learning.

I looked in the back and there was a hole in the door, down under the window. It was shredded around the opening. The hole was little, but bullets are not that big. I thought about the ones in the news photos. Just little holes, but ones that went all the way through.

"They shot us? The army?"

"No the army would just open up with an automatic. This was someone else. And just warning us, I think. The villagers here know how to use guns. The shooter missed the engine and the fuel tank and us, so he was careful. He only shot once and we left. Or we were lucky."

Everyone kept telling me how lucky I was. It wasn't the army this time; it wasn't the drug gangs last time. I wasn't feeling lucky, though. If I were lucky, I would be sitting down in the pueblo having a big lunch with the townsfolk. That was the luck I wanted.

The car banged on a rock. I ducked.

"We should be safe now." I guessed Efraím would know. But he drove us out to get shot at near the mine.

I left Efraím to his driving. He took a side road around the pueblo that required a lot of swerving and dodging for the rocks. I was thinking about dodging bullets. I wished you could dodge them, like they do in the movies, in slow motion. This was the first time bullets came at me. With the

Colonel, they went the other way. I liked that better. But then the Colonel didn't.

We drove through the pueblo´s blockade again. It was open and the men were back by the cliff wall. Efraím waved. They stared at us, or maybe just at me. After we passed he slowed and started driving normally, a bit too fast for me, but normal for him. Finally, after a long half hour, we reached the highway.

I figured he would talk then. "OK, what's happening?" I asked.

"Roberto, my friend, you are a good friend. This is a complicated place. It would take all day to explain. But I will tell you what you need to know. That is better for you. In case your Señor Ruiz or maybe the Police Captain asks."

He was looking straight ahead. Efraím always knew a lot more than he told. I was one of his sources. I told him about the expats. He listened. He listened to many people. And he watched.

In exchange, he told me funny stories about people and Oaxaca. It had always seemed like a fair trade. He knew a whole lot more than he ever let on. Now he knew things I needed to know.

"There are groups who don't want my pueblo's people around the mine site. People from another pueblo that wants to control the site. They want to control access, but the road goes through our pueblo. I think they were warning us to get back. I did not think they would shoot if a gringo was riding along in my taxi. I was wrong."

Is that was why he wanted me? A shield. One that did not work very well. One that might get holes in it? He was wrong about the shield. Everyone was wrong recently. They told me everything would go back to normal after the assassination, it did not. They told me I was fine, and now I was really worrying.

"Another pueblo? They were the ones who shot at us?"

"They just warned us. It was my poor car they shot. But it is in no pain. It is a tough taxi. All is well."

Efraím could dance around with words but this time I wanted a straight line to the truth. "What pueblo?"

"It is over the hill, a little farther from the mining site than ours. We sometimes argue over water or over cattle straying, but this gold has made life more difficult."

"I thought that this was a fight with the mining company."

"You gringos want things simple. Down here many people are struggling. Maybe up there in el Norte it is the same? In addition to the pueblos and the mining company and the government, there is probably a miners union and of course the teachers union will have its say. And the political parties, of course. And don't forget the foreigners. They have the final word. That word is money."

"Things are not two sided, not black and white like you believe. With God on your side and the devil everywhere else. Down here everyone knows the devil can be sitting on your shoulder, even on our side, the good side. All good Catholics know that."

I thought for a minute. About Ruiz fighting with the ex-Governor and the dinosaur politicians and using me. And about Efraím. My friend had a little of the dark streak in him, a devil on his shoulder. He would like some of the gold for his 401K. Hell, I would too. I needed to know more.

"What happened to the man from the Trout Farm?"

"No one knows. He was at the barricade, all alone, because of some screw up in the schedule. And then he was gone. A couple days later he turned up above the Trout Farm, dead. That is all I know. Maybe the ex-Governor took him for a ride. A little warning."

Efraím seemed like he was leveling with me. But he had lots of levels. I think I had moved up one. Or maybe down to the first basement to where the deeper secrets are stored. I needed to go down one more level and ask my hardest question. I had been thinking about it for a while.

"Why did we go to the Trout Farm that day?"

"You were hungry. Remember."

"But I started out heading to an Angus restaurant. Somehow we ended up on the fish trip. You talked me into it."

Efraím thought for a second. "Yes, you are right. I wanted to see the mountain, above the Trout Farm, but I didn't know about the murder. And you like fish. I knew that. I wanted you there as cover in case anyone saw me up on the mountain. You gringos make good cover. We can duck behind you. You are too big for your own good."

"But why did you want to see it."

"I had heard rumors. About gold. You know how much gold is worth these days?"

He was smiling. He was using me. I used him, too. Maybe that was part of our friendship. I opened the door to see the expat-Americans and he opened the window on

181

Oaxaca. But I like to think friendship is more than just a trade.

"So what now?" I was wondering what could be next, what could be worse than the killing in the village.

"Let's eat goat. It's right up the road."

I had forgotten about the *birria*, Jalisco-style *birria*. I had not forgotten about food for years.

Cerveza

Efraím shook me. A big meal after two hectic days of flying, going to the mine, and getting shot at had worn me out. Goat is heavy, especially when drowned in a fatty sauce with tortillas and beer. I slept an hour in the taxi coming back from Efraím's pueblo.

"Siesta is over. You are home." Efraím shook me.

I yawned and looked around. We were on my street. The bougainvillea was starting to lose its red flowers. The day was fuzzy but coming back. Then I remembered.

"What are we going to do about your pueblo, about the dead guy, about the Trout Farm, about …"

"Sleep on it. I will let you know what happens soon."

My sidekick duties were over. "You know I am around if you need anything." I called out. I couldn't think of anything useful he or his pueblo or anyone down here could want from me, except for me to stand in front of them, being a gringo shield if things got nasty. I was not sure I wanted to do that.

"Be careful, Efraím, You know you owe me a dinner. I plan to collect so don't get any bullet holes in you, or machete chops, either. I bought lunch today. You owe me for that. And for getting me shot at."

"You be careful too. You might have a heart attack after eating like that. But before you go too far, I have to tell you that something is about to happen. I cannot go into details. Watch out."

He reached out the window towards me and I tried to do one of those fancy handshakes with a knuckle bump and slide that the taxistas do. I messed it up. Efraím just wacked my fist. "You are almost there, Señor Gringo. You just need to practice the taxista fist bump a little more."

He drove off. As I turned to the house, Maria came running out. I was worried, but she said I there had been a message on the phone. She gave me the note, written in the Señora's beautiful script. Arturo called wanting me to meet him for *almuerzo*, a late breakfast, tomorrow. His daughter's church group was dancing by the cathedral at 12:30.

That takes care of tomorrow, I thought, but not quite time to call the day quits yet. I still had something to do. I went to a pay phone stand across the street and called Randy´s cell up in San Francisco. It was a spur of the minute thing, but I did plan a little. I called on the street pay phone because I was not feeling secure about my cell or even chatting on my computer. How much power did Ruiz have down here? And who could his silent partners be? The new Governor? Maybe he could get a copy of everything I said? I was thinking maybe the pay phone was too close to my apartment and ready hang up to go to one even farther away when Randy answered. We did not do any catching up, she just jumped into the news.

"He is going to settle. I am sure. But first, a fuss. He is holding out, I don't know why but your Lupe will be a wealthy young mama."

My Lupe? Oh, well.

Randy told me more about the lawyer´s negotiations, about her plans for worker protection for the doctor's house and office, and the size of the payout they were trying for. Well, Lupe and Baby-Beto might get something but they were not going to be really wealthy, but a lot better off than most of us expats. I guess that would be a good ending for this part of the story. But it was still being negotiated, she reminded me.

I paused. I felt tentative but went ahead. "Can you help me? I need some information about mines down here in Oaxaca."

"You are not digging coal mines again?"

I was fighting against the mines this time. I was on Randy's side. Well mostly. I did not know how to explain my conversion. Because they killed my Trout Farm? That did not sound much like a conversion. I was ready to be the Saint Paul of the miners and go over, but I did not get into that with Randy. It was too complicated for a phone call. Saint Paul wrote a bunch of chapters to explain his conversion. I only had two minutes on a phone.

"It is mixed up with that picture that Lupe had of me. Remember? I want to know if I am in trouble. But I need to know who is involved. Can you ask one of your friends to help?"

I told her about the mines, the one with the dead guy and the other one where the dead guy was buried today. She was giving me an "oh no" with each new part of the story but she didn't interrupt. "I need to know the Mexican contact running interference for the mining corporations down here."

Randy understood under the table deals. They happened in West Virginia. They probably happened everywhere. She would know where to get the info. But would she trust me with it?

A big rain drop hit me on top of the head. Others followed.

"I am getting wet. It's raining. I've got to run." I thanked her, sent a hug and hung up. It started really raining, not just an afternoon shower, so I ran to the door and fumbled for the key.

I got in and wanted to go numb for a while. Maybe a good book, but not a murder mystery tonight, and a cerveza or two to keep me company. Something to blot out the bullet hole that came after me today, the bullet before the *birria* and after the roadblock.

Sunday

Pan Dulce

They shot at me. That was my first thought when I woke up. It was the last part of a dream with lots of fast driving and bullets zinging by. Not my normal Oaxaca sleep, when the only threat was small, buzzing, and trying to suck a little blood. I thought back to those hated mosquito nights and how much better they were than ones with lead flying around.

It was early when sat up. I was waiting for something, but not sure what it was. Efraím warned me something was cooking. I saw no end to this mess and was worried that my Oaxaca days were ending. My peaceful days already had ended.

I dressed and went out. The rain that poured last night had slackened, now more of a heavy drizzle. The empty streets smelled fresh for a change, and glistened, cheering me a bit. Church bells did their Sunday duty waking everyone who worked all week and needed to sleep in another hour or two. Startled pigeons flew from the church roof every time the bells started up. The flock circled overhead and then resettled on their old perches when the bells stopped.

I went towards the cathedral where Arturo would meet me in four hours. Only a couple people walked on the street, heavily bundled, waterproofed and cold looking. I did my warm-blooded gringo act and walked by smiling in my shirt sleeves, but under an umbrella. The people I passed tucked themselves into doorways like they did not want me to see them. Or maybe they just were avoiding the morning wetness.

I went to a roof-covered restaurant patio next to the cathedral, in front of a hotel that had been around a long time. The décor had not changed much ever; it made you think of Oaxaca a century ago. You paid double for this fantasy, but were waited on by waitresses in full, starched skirts that looked like something a colonial governor would have wanted his servants to wear. The walls surrounded you with dusty pictures of Oaxacan streets that had no cars, only a few burros and a wooden cart or two. Perfect for a slow, wet Sunday.

Today, in the rain, this was the one place you could watch the cathedral, sit dry, and have coffee and pastries. Everywhere else had big umbrellas and tarps stretched above the tables, dripping rain down on the food. I went upscale. Dry sounded good, even if it cost a little.

I looked for the human traffic on the street, but mostly watched the trees branches blowing, because not many people were out that early. Rain did not slow the local people, but none hurried until the tourists came out, and the tourists were staying warm and dry in their beds this Sunday.

A pair of men, not right for the place and time, walked up and sat on the side of the patio. They were too big and too bulky and too slick looking. They looked at me but turned when I looked back. I was getting that feeling. The one I read about in detective novels when the hero was being followed. When his hair stands up.

Then another pair sat on the other side, looking like twins of the first two guys. All four had long raincoats that could hide not just a pistol but a couple shotguns each. They started looking at each other, not friendly looks, but looks like they knew each other in a bad sort of way.

The waitress came and took orders and everything calmed but I had the feeling something was happening, like Efraím had said. It seemed safest to stay put and see if they were watching me or if I was just a bystander to some kind of standoff between them. I checked for places to jump behind the hotel's stone wall, just in case.

We five were the only customers. We all had coffee and tried not to look at each other. At least, that was what I did.

I was not sure who these two groups of guys were, but I seemed to be attracting them. Like roadkill does to gangster crows. And they did not seem to like each other. I was not sure if the game today was new Governor vs. old Gov, feds vs. thugs, or maybe gold mine vs. gold mine. But I was pretty sure no one was on my side. Well, maybe the waitress, but she stayed mostly in the kitchen.

After three *pan dulces* and two coffees for me and a coffee or two for them, one pair stood. They walked down to the plaza and looked back, not at me, but at the others. Then they turned deliberately, showing their backs as they walked slowly to a bench sheltered by one of the big laurel trees.

They were working for position, like chess players. I was a pawn, at the most, so I took the opportunity to jump up and leave by a side exit. I went into the cathedral. That seemed safer than the patio. I did not look back.

Mass was going on. The priest was speaking, electronically amplified into a pleasant unintelligible babble. It could have been Latin, for all everyone understood. I sat with a group of old women and looked back at the door when we knelt. No big men came in. Maybe it was not me they were looking for, but like the faithful, I was looking for signs. The bullet in the taxi and the men following me were all the signs I needed to know that my days in Oaxaca were almost over. I couldn't live looking over my shoulder.

Arturo and his family showed up at one. I was still sitting in the pew. Mass had ended and the cathedral emptied except for me and a few lost tourists trying to find something worth snapping a picture of. They soon realized that this building was not for them. The gold-covered church, Santo Domingo, the touristy one, was a couple blocks away. The cathedral was grey, damp and only for the faithful or the dead—the ones sleeping under the stone floor.

I watched Arturo's family enter and pray. That was the joy of Oaxaca. People believed and God rewarded them by

190

hanging around and keeping an eye on them, except not for us expats or politicians. We were on our own. God watched the city people struggle and die, but he hung heaven over their heads, like a promise to children for ice cream if they were good.

Arturo greeted me. He wanted me to see his family again. There was no purpose in the visit, other than just seeing each other, renewing the glue between us. He didn't have any news. Didn't really want to talk much. Just wanted me to know they cared and understood this was a hard time for me. People here understood hard times.

The ground was wet outside the cathedral and the rain was coming down, not hard but steady. The daughter's folkloric event went on. It takes more than rain to stop dancing and music in Oaxaca. She wore a big plastic bag over her embroidered dress. The dancing was energetic. That's enough when you are young. It was patriotic, not artistic. For teenage Mexicans, folk dance tied them to history. No butt-shaking, pop dancing here, only the same footwork and swirls that had been going on hundreds of years. It was good to watch. Like a mind cleaning. I needed one after watching breakfast with thugs a couple hours earlier.

I decided not to tell Arturo what had happened with Efraím and the guys watching me this morning. Arturo needed to keep living in Oaxaca. I could leave, even Efraím could run, but Arturo was rooted with family, faith, work, and everything Mexican. And he knew too much already. I did not want him in trouble.

I hugged his family, not sure if it was a goodbye. I kept that to myself. They headed home and to their life. I walked away.

I looked around for the big men from the morning. The square was crowded and warmer. No one was wearing heavy coats any more. The rain had let up and only looked threatening. A couple men were getting shoe shines. A couple more were standing and smoking near the walk behind the church where children played with balloons.

I finally called it quits and gave up on sighting my thugs. I did not want to see them anyway. I walked home fast. Not looking back, not thinking much. Just thinking about which suitcase to take on the plane if I had to high-tail it to the States.

Snickers

Monday did not get better. It was raining hard again. I got up late and walked to the American library, really cold this time and bundled up like everyone else. I hoped Carlos was there. I know he gets on my nerves, but he was the legal expert. He thought he knew everything. Of course, that was why he got on my nerves, but he did know Mexican laws and helped us fill out those long forms that the government tortured us with when we wanted to be Mexicans residents.

"Roberto, you are soaked. What are you doing out when the hurricane is coming? It has already hit the coast and will be climbing up the mountains dumping its rain." Carlos and Lark were sitting behind one of the tables. "We are all going to be underwater tomorrow. They are not talking about inches, but a foot of water."

"I will get my poncho and boots out." A hurricane–that was why this weather was so crazy. I was out of contact with the world. Their world, I mean. I was in much too close contact with my own crazy gold and dead fish world.

We did our hugs. I included Lark this time. She was now part of the gang. I had hoped to get Carlos alone, but that was not going to happen anymore. The two were glued.

I looked at Carlos and went ahead, "I need to know about last year when the police got your name. How did that get straightened out?" I didn't mention that he was marching with Linda who got in front of every group taking to the streets to reform Oaxaca. Linda had been replaced.

He stared. "Well, I don't do that anymore. And they don't bother me. It sort of faded. No harm, no penalty." I figured his new lady Lark was less of a marcher.

I thought he had paid off someone. Or did something lawyerly. But he just did the quiet gringo act and it all went away.

Lark spoke up, "you know the rules, and follow them, and you are ok."

I wish that were true. I followed all the rules and look at me. OK, I broke a couple, but that was for Lupe and not in Mexico anyway.

"Are you having problems?" Carlos looked concerned. Probably it was the look he used with his clients in the old days. "Just take it easy and do the tourist thing. Maybe climb the pyramids or go swimming on the beach. That was what I did. You never know who you will meet." Lark smiled at him. That line was for her, not me.

"I am just trying to understand how things work down here, especially after that shooting." They nodded at me.

"Yes, your Colonel. He was a problem." Carlos paused a second and this time he smiled at Lark. Like he would explain something to her later. "Now you take care of yourself. Lark and I have to go before the full hurricane gets here. It won't be too windy but will rain like hell."

Not much help. I walked up to the snack bar and picked up a Snickers. That was my comida so far for the day. I had sunk pretty low.

I was not ready to leave Oaxaca yet. I loved it in Oaxaca. I just needed some time to figure this out.

I wandered over to the bulletin board: lots of mind-stretching yoga, lost cats, cheap therapy and healing cures. Nothing to help me. The library was always full of new age offers, most a generation behind what was happening in the States. Now in the States you had hot box yoga and "Rich Dad, Poor Dad" weekends and, even worse, the noxious money woman´s endless TV seminars. I did not want to go back and be one of the poor dads. I preferred lost cats and cold yoga down here.

One ad was posted by someone heading back. Or maybe scared back, who knew? Their ad was long: refrigerators, mattresses, car, phones, plants, everything for sale. "All must go by Thursday."

I had to get out of the library. Just to ride around and find some fresh air. I took the first cab that went by. He asked where. I gave him the address in the ad for the refrigerator and mattress. I wondered what their story was.

The cab left the Centro area. We entered one of the poorer barrios. Potholes got bigger, walls had more graffiti. Electric wires hung down in tangles, looking like nests for some robot birds. The wires were bunched up on the concrete poles, fat bunches that grew bigger when old wires were cut down and left dangling and new, maybe illegal, ones put up. I could reach up and touch them, they hung so low.

We passed old men riding bicycles. We passed small shops with the basics: tortillas, eggs and beans. Street vendors huddling under umbrellas sold home-made sweets out of wooden carts. Boys, wrapped in plastic sheets, called out the things they carried, candy and cigarettes, all neatly arranged in their wooden boxes hung around their necks, to sell to kids and poor men, one smoke at a time. We passed no beggars. It did not pay out here.

Cars were older in this barrio. A couple cars passed us. One had children hanging out the back window and I turned to watch them as their car went by. As I was looking back at the kids I noticed, right behind us, a big car tailgating my cab. Like it wanted to pass and was getting ready. But it just hung behind.

It didn't belong here in this barrio. It was a shiny, black SUV, an extra large one like politicians used. And behind it, another. Two men were in the first. I could see them through the windshield. I could not tell anything about the second one, except it looked evil, like those assassin cars in the movies.

I got the cabbie to u-turn fast. The two SUVs did tricky spins, like TV cops. I tried to see inside the cars as they spun around, but you could not see anything through their dark side windows. They are so dark I bet they couldn't see out much either. The cars were not even trying to hide from me. I couldn't believe it. Time to buy plane tickets and kiss my Oaxaca goodbye? Unfortunately yes.

The cab took me home. I quit looking back at the cars. They had not tried to stop us. I did not know what they were doing. Maybe just scaring me. Letting me know they were there.

I zeroed in on getting to the door of my house. But as I got there, the Señora and Lupe came out. I pushed the cab door open in front of them and started to warn them, but the black SUVs were gone.

I hugged the two women like I had not seen them for a long time. It did seem like a long time. Getting chased can make you old fast.

Bells for mass were ringing. The Señora was herding Lupe into religion now that she lived in the house, walking her to mass every day. Maria went every other day. The Señora worked out a compromise with God to get more work done in the house and still keep Maria ready for heaven.

I went with them watching out for the SUVs. I wanted to say goodbye because I was pretty sure I would be leaving soon. Probably the next day. I could get tickets at the airport. But for a few minutes, now that the SUVs had gone, I just wanted to enjoy being near them, to remember them. The three of us walked down the street. The afternoon sun was low and coming thru a couple holes in the clouds. The rain had stopped for a few minutes. I took the Señora's arm, held her umbrella and we walked to the church. The two women would go in and get on their knees. I would go back and pack. We talked about simple things, the weather and flowers and the new priest, things she used to talk about before the Colonel entered my life.

Then I saw the red car. Not one of those that had followed me. This one was old, dented and driving fast, up on the sidewalk where we were walking, twenty five yards away, coming at us. I grabbed at the women to push them against the wall but there was no place to go. I was about to pull them in the street, sure we would all be flattened in a second. That was when the Señora´s Virgin upstairs, started working. The car bounced in the open manhole in the sidewalk, the one that always was trying to break my leg, the one I cursed and was going to fill with rocks one night. Then the red car bounced out of the manhole, careened off the wall and skidded into the street, going past us, missing by a foot or so, and sliding on the wet cobblestones, going sideways toward the big hole that workmen had left in center of the street. A caution tape was all that kept cars away and it snapped as the red car went through.

I never had been happy that all work got done slowly here in Oaxaca. In the States holes would have been filled in a day. Worksites here last a long time and sometimes stay forever. But I will pray for slowness in everything from now on.

The car dropped nose down in the hole with a crash and a breaking glass crunch. The driver bounced against the windshield and then did not move. His horn blared. He lay on top of the steering wheel. I ran around and saw the spider web of glass that his head punched in the windshield. It was dripping red. Another picture for the newspaper tomorrow, like the one of the Colonel.

The car had been heading for me, a whack job, like the one with the Colonel. The SUVs were not just following me, they were setting me up. Everything Arturo and Efraím and everyone else had said was wrong, I was not safe. The SUVs were not scaring me; they were trying to get me.

The Señora looked over at the car and the unconscious driver. She held Lupe. The Señora's son, Jorge came running out the door.

"He tried to kill me," I yelled. "He was driving up the sidewalk, aiming the car at me." Then I added, "and at your mother and Lupe."

Young men from the neighborhood ran toward the car. The Señora called for them to grab the driver and pull him out. Soon he was lying on the street, moving his head a little and bleeding a lot.

You son of a whore, or something like that, the young men yelled. One threw the driver an old rag to press on his bleeding face. Everyone was calling him a murderer. The crowd of men started kicking him.

"You tried to kill my mother, *cabron*," Jorge joined in and gave him a good kick.

Then without any planning the men grabbed the driver and carried him over to a tree. Someone had a rope and I was scared I was going to see a lynching. The Señora calmly said to tie him up. They did, about ten feet up in the tree; so that if he struggled, he would slide down making the ropes tighter. Some ropes were around his neck.

I was yelling too. "Who hired you to come after me. Who was it?" I was even madder than when my fish restaurant died. Or when the Colonel's son was crying.

"Who are you?" he croaked back at me with a voice squeezed by the rope. He stared at me like I was from another planet.

That was when Señora took over the interrogation, doing it slowly like the Jesuits during the inquisition before they burned you at the stake. She had encouragement from the crowd that picked up shovels and rocks around the work site where the car was sitting nose down.

He confessed. He was not trying to hit me with the car. He was aiming at the pregnant Lupe, not at me.

I was not a target. I was relieved, except he would have hit me and killed me too. The Señora started praying, calling on God for justice and asking who paid him. A couple whacks with the shovel and the killer in the tree confessed some more. He was paid off by a cousin living in LA in some gang who got money from a doctor. A doctor who sent him the ten thousand pesos in his pocket. The Señora and I knew which doctor.

Mentioning the States set the Señora off and she yelled at the driver until he turned white and his tongue was hanging out the side of his mouth. The ropes were cutting deeper into his neck.

It took a while for the police and priest to free the driver because no one dared stop the Señora. I thought she was going to hit him with the shovel. She knew she would be forgiven at next confession and did not worry about earthly laws. She had her connections here. She had connections above. She explained that to me many times.

After an hour or so, the priest from down the street arranged for the men to hand the driver to the police. They did not want to let him go.

The police pulled the rope free. The driver fell to the concrete and the police held him up. It was over. The Señora said something I never heard before. She called the doctor in LA a son of a dog. She was going to need her confession tonight.

I had mixed feelings. No one was after me, but the doctor was after Lupe. I was sure I was free from being chased. I started laughing. Laughing too much. The Señora walked over. She looked concerned and she shook me, softly.

"Now stop. Lupe and Maria will see you. Then what will they do after seeing you like that."

I stopped, not wanting to cross this lady. Instead, I hugged everyone again. I thought it was over.

But then, as I bent over Lupe to hug her, I looked down the street and there was the black SUV again, one block away. Two men leaned against the door, not looking at me. They had their eyes on something else. I turned around and a block over on the other side was another SUV. Two more men were watching from there, not watching me so much as the other car.

The eyeballing match that I saw in front of the cathedral in the morning had resumed in full swing. I was wondering whether to duck under a car or run inside the apartment when a police car, light flashing and siren blaring, turned the corner and started coming at us. That should have scared the SUVs, but they did not move. You never knew who was in charge here. It definitely was not the police.

The police car stopped in front of me but left the siren and lights running. The back door opened and the police captain who had interrogated me about the Colonel the week before, when all this mess started, got out. He still had his hat pulled down tight and his military style uniform buttoned much too tight.

"Señor Evans, you must come with me, now."

That seemed better than waiting for one of the SUVs to come for me, so I got in with him. He said nothing and we went back to the station where I had spent three hours on the morning the Colonel died.

We started out with the basics. Where did I live, how long, what kind of passport did I have. They skipped all this the first time. Then we went back over the Colonel's shooting. I had the same story. That was easy. Then he hit me with the hard question. "Why did you go to the gold field near the Trout Farm on the day that Juan Ezekiel Rodriguez was killed?"

That was the first time I had heard his name. I had my story ready. It was easy because it was true. "I went for fish but they were closed at the Trout Farm."

"Then why did you go to the funeral?"

I thought as fast as I could. "I had heard about the murder. I wanted to pray for the man killed near where I had been. I also prayed for the Colonel when he was shot. I pray a lot these days."

This was true. I prayed for the boy and I prayed at the village funeral. Praying over the dead man released me a little from the image of him lying next to the stream. His image had been stuck in my head but it loosened up after I prayed hard to send him on his way.

I played dumb gringo at the police station. It was not hard. I did not know what was happening. But I left out Efraím and his cab and I left out going to see the new mine of Señor Ruiz and I left out the bullet hole. I was trying hard to remember all the things I was leaving out, so I could just be a simple, scared expat telling his very true story.

Anyway, I was not scared of the police. I was scared of what would happen if I walked out of the police station and the SUVs were around.

"Señor Evans, we need to check out your statement. While we do so, you must stay here. You are not under arrest so you do not need to call your government."

They marched me away quickly. They said I was just being detained, not arrested. Some technical difference. But I got the same size cell. They walked me down the hall and down the stairs and finally to a room that had a lock looking like it belonged in a museum. The jailer had a key that matched it. He pushed me in and slammed the door. It clanged just like in the movies.

I had a bench and a bucket. That was it. I sat down and put my head down. This was not my plan for the night. And my stomach growled. The Snickers—that was it for me—it looked like no food here tonight.

I sat on the bench an hour or two. Men were yelling and then suddenly silent. That was scary. There was no water. The bucket did not count. I did not want to know what was in there. I did not complain. I kept still, staring at the barely lit wall. Sitting here was a great way to feel like you lived longer. Time went slow. Or maybe did not move at all.

I reviewed everything I had said to the police. It was all true. I just left out things. They had nothing on me. My story was that I was hungry for fish and then I was upset about the dead man. No crime. I should get out soon as I called the consul. Whenever they let me. I was pretty sure they did that down here. I should have checked more with Carlos. Maybe the consul will come and get me.

I heard footsteps on the concrete. They clomped down the walk and stopped in front of my door. It opened and I saw two men. One was the jailer with his keys; the other was a man in a suit way too expensive for any consul staff.

"Señor Evans there has been a horrible confusion. The police were not allowed to detain you. I have corrected it. You may leave." The jailer looked over at the man in the suit after the man finished speaking.

I was ready to run out the cell's door before they changed their minds but I wanted to know who this man was. Maybe he drove a black SUV and had a long ride waiting for me. Or worse, a short ride.

"I have been asked by Señor Ruiz to take you home. He sends his apologies."

"But the police…"

"The police are confused. Señor Ruiz appreciated the help you gave him and wants you to know that this sort of thing cannot happen to his friends. So you are free. Let us go. I will drive you home."

I did not really want the ride, but it looked like an offer that I could not turn down.

As we walked out the building I thought the police would bow down to the man leading me. He had pull. Or rather his boss did. He never did give a name. He took me to his Mercedes, it was white, so I felt a little better about this ride. At least it was not one of the SUVs. The driver opened the door. We got in the back. The man beside me said nothing more. I thanked him two or three times and finally realized that this was a good time for silence.

The driver ran a couple pedestrians back to the curb and ignored the traffic lights and stop signs. We were at my house in record time.

"Señor Ruiz wants to see you tomorrow at noon. A car will pick you up. There have been some developments that he wants to talk to you about."

"Sure." What else could I say?

I looked down the street. Someone had pulled the red crashed car away. The big hole was just sitting there waiting for another car. I wanted to throw some holy water on it for saving me.

Maria came out and hugged me. When I went through the door and Lupe approached and started crying. The Señora and her son joined us. "What have you done? They say you are a killer."

That was not good. Her son handed me the evening paper. The headline was in extra large type, "American Hacks Miner to Death for Gold."

"It was not me. They made a mistake. These are lies."

The Señora crossed herself. "I knew it was wrong. They print lies all the time. I prayed and that is why you are free. Let us go to the altar and thank the Virgin."

I was ready to thank anyone for being out and free. I had originally planned to thank Señor Ruiz when we met the next day, but it was probably better to thank the Virgin right now. Fewer strings attached with her.

I left the family after they all declared their faith in my innocence. I took the paper up the stairs and read it in my room.

> A money-crazed American, Robert Evans, took a cab to the old gold mine on Highway 175 past the pueblo of Huayapam, and silently came up behind Juan Ezequiel Rodriguez. The villain Evans hit Rodriguez on the head with an ax handle and grabbed his bag of gold powder, the results of months of work at the old mine. Rodriguez resisted vigorously. The immigrant thief then grabbed a machete and stuck Rodriguiez, once, twice, three times, finally severing part of his head. The injured man fell at the crazed killer´s feet. The recently severed artery sprayed blood on the clothes of the killer. He fled running. He was seen throwing out bloodstained clothes by a maid who lived near his house.

Wait, I threw out my clothes from when the Colonel was shot. It is wrong, They just made all this up.

I was reading the *Sección Roja*. It had the picture of the body on the mountain. It had a photograph of me from the day the Colonel was killed. They had gone crazy.

I ran down to tell the family again.

"This is lies. There is nothing true. You must believe me."

"Of course it is lies. They do this all the time. If someone important asks them, they write a story. They had one story about a neighbor who had done nothing. And there was nothing our neighbor could do to punish the paper. The newspaper has friends like the judge and the ex-Governor."

They had real freedom of the press down here.

"You cannot do much. Unless you call another paper, one with friends like the new Governor, and have them write another story about you and maybe about how the ex-Governor is out to get you. I do not know how you became his enemy, but he is one to watch out for. He and his friends. Things are difficult now that we have a new Governor and they are changing the heads of all the departments. They are angry. Be careful."

They did not need to tell me. I was watching every shadow and looking to see if the doors were locked. I wanted to check the barbed wire running along the top of the wall and dangle raw meat over the dog to make him mad. Anything to be safe tonight, and then fly out tomorrow.

"I must rest. This has been a difficult day."

The Señora gave me another of her blessings, Maria gave me a hug and Lupe started crying–the same family script that we had gone through before. I went upstairs and took a long shower. I was lucky, no one yelled I was using all the water that night.

I lay down half wet and fell immediately asleep.

Gansitos

God, I was hungry.

It was grey. The rain was pouring down again. The hurricane had hit but I was still alive. That was all I asked for. And some food. I rummaged through my cupboard and found a pack of Gansitos, the closest things to Twinkies that Mexicans made. I gobbled a couple and took a long swig from a bottle of water that had been sitting on my desk a while. Then a couple more Gansitos. My diet had gone to hell since all this started.

I was wondering whether to get dressed when Maria came running up the stairs. "It is a phone call." I came down with my pants mostly up and answered. Randy was on the line.

"What did you do?" she yelled.

"It is all lies. I did not kill the dead miner. He was dead when I got there."

"I am not talking about a miner; I mean the doctor in LA. Someone burned his house and killed his dogs. They all got roasted in the fire. They were his show dogs, but more like his children from what I hear, except he had ten or twenty of them. But, maybe he hid away a bunch of human kids too, with the way he chased his maids and the women at his office."

"Killed his dogs? That is bad."

You could kill people in the States and, if it was only one or two, there was not much fuss. Especially if you could claim they were in gangs, did drugs or were from Mexico. That was the way it was. But killing dogs always made the front page. The doctor´s news was probably on every TV station in the US with lots of cute dead puppy videos.

"They were those god-awful, ugly, hairless Mexican dogs. Not even Chihuahuas. They were the big ones that Indians used to eat. Now they are all dead. Roasted. Well done. Barbecued. And the house is gone too. The doctor and his wife are OK. Just crying on TV this morning about their puppy babies."

I was thinking they probably had the whole FBI out on this one.

"You could see the fire from downtown LA. I don't know what they used to start it but it was big. They said it had to be arson. The police just came here to see me. They wanted to know about Lupe and the doctor. I have my lawyer talking to them."

Shit, the police were after Randy. I did not know what to tell her. I certainly was not going to talk about the red car chasing Lupe yesterday.

"I don't know anything. Someone was angry at him. Maybe the doctor mistreated others too. Maybe he had lots of enemies."

"That was what I told the police. I do not want to know any more about what you are doing down there. You seem to have a mafia and I want to stay out of it."

I thought about how angry the Señora was yesterday. How she looked like she was ready kill that driver after he nearly ran down Lupe and her unborn baby. And what she called the doctor. The Señora had her phone and that network of hers. I knew it went up to Mexico City and from there who knew how far north. And the Señora was tough. Maybe her friends were even tougher. I won't ask. Randy was right, this was something better not to know about.

Randy broke the silence, "Now, I will tell you what I learned about the gold. After that, let's not talk for a while. I want to just let this rest."

She shuffled some pages, probably getting some notes to read. "The mine ownership you asked about is being contested in court in Mexico. It seems that the ex-Governor controlled mineral rights and had a deal with a Canadian company, Ore Exchange, Ltd., but after the election when the ex-Governor left for the States, a new Mexican group, with ties to the new Governor has been challenging the ex-Governor's ownership. They are working with same Canadian company. Just changing the Mexican end. The only name I could get was some front man for the new group, Alfonzo Ruiz. And that other mine, the one up the mountain, where you said the dead man was found, it was under direct control of Ruiz's group."

Ruiz. Was Alfonzo his first name? God, I get names mixed up. It had to be him. I have his card somewhere or I could double check it when I see him. And it was his mine up by the Trout Farm. Shit! I had better go see him even if I am flying out later. He might try to stop me. Stop me in a bad way.

"Thank you, Randy." I was sweating hard and it was not hot. Our conversion needed some repair. "I have not done anything bad. Please believe me. I am just trapped in a crazy fight down here. One I walked into just going down the street. But I will be out of it soon." I did not tell her about coming back. I would do that when I got there.

"We can talk more later. In a couple weeks. Take care of yourself." She was abrupt and hung up. That was a rough start for the day and now I had to go see Ruiz.

I tried to fit in this latest information from Randy and add it to what Arturo and Efraím had told me. There were the old politicos headed by the ex-Governor, the ones they call dinosaurs down here, and the new ones who supported the new Governor. The old dinosaurs bumped off the Colonel, I think. Maybe the Colonel switched sides. Ruiz was with the Colonel's family and it looks like Ruiz was on the new Governor´s side. I think. And the new ones must be taking over the gold mine from the old ones. They liked money just as much as the old dinosaurs. Maybe they were dinosaurs too. Just in new clothes. Who knows?

Then Ephraim's village was fighting the other village and Juan from the village was dead and who knows which side did that. The Trout Farm mine was involved too. That was Ruiz' mine. But everyone says it has no gold left in it. One thing for sure, everyone is after gold.

And the doctor from LA with his dead Mexican dogs was after Lupe. That was the kind of settlement he wanted, not one with a lawyer. But the doctor seemed to be from another story.

I was on Ephraim's side in all this, and I guess that his friends were my friends. I was not sure if there was a good or a bad side anymore, just friends and enemies and maybe some people in between. Like Arturo who tried to ride through all this and make sure water came out of the pipes for the people down here, whoever won.

Ruiz got me out of jail so maybe he was on my side, or maybe he was using me. Maybe everyone was using me. And it looked like the ex-Governor was dead set against me. A lot of people were following me. Maybe people from both sides. I needed a chart for all this.

I had time for breakfast before Ruiz. I was hungry. That was the one thing I knew for sure. I needed something to keep the Gansitos company in my stomach, so I walked to La Avenida.

Oaxaca was beautiful, like always, but it was wet. Rain was coming down hard and some of the drains backed up making rivers in the older streets. But it was also cleaning off the buildings and making the air sweet and making me wish I were still in a head-in-the-sand tourist wonderland, the one I knew a couple weeks back, not in this goldmine rat's nest.

I was dodging puddles, thinking about Oaxaca. That was why I forgot to look around to see if anyone was following me. Starting new habits is hard, even if they are good for you, like looking both ways across the street to see if someone is waiting to bump you off.

A man in a suit came up next to me before I noticed him. I did a deer-in-the-headlights jump for a second watching to see what he pulled out from his suit coat, but he only pulled out a piece of paper, not a gun. He read it, and called out my name in a syrupy southern USA accent. Maybe I should not have said, "That's me." But I did and the man pulled me aside to a sheltered spot away from the rain.

"Mister Evans, a moment please." He spoke his Alabama English. "Mee-istur" was really what he said. I would hate to hear him speaking Spanish. His long sagging vowels would be at war with the precise ones you need in Spanish.

"I am Donald Price from the American Consulate. Call me Don. I have a message for you." It took him a long time to get that out.

When all the vowels were finished I was smiling. I was thanking the Virgin that he was not don dinosaur executioner from the ex-Gov. He had not been in Mexico long. You could tell because no one official goes to first names that fast in Mexico. You have to put your degrees out too to be respected. He must have been a new flunky for the consulate.

I wanted to ask him if his message was about my evening in the jail and whether he could have gotten me out as fast as Ruiz did, but I was working on being silent, being Mexicano.

"Can we go someplace private?" He did not want to be out on the street talking. I did not care anymore. I just wanted to be dry. And it was pretty wet out in the rain. But maybe it was better to be as public as possible when you were being stalked.

"Can I see your ID, Don?" My new American friend was real. He was official. At least his ID was, or maybe a good fake.

I started thinking that anyone could make a badge that looked that official on a computer these days, but I had survived him so far and wanted to see what he had to say—he might be some help–so I took him to the back corner of La Avenida.

Everyone there, Carlos and Lark included, were looking at us. This was my first time out since the newspaper story appeared, writing that I was the murderer who killed the dead-fish miner with a machete. I was sure I was the hot expat topic this morning. They must have been wondering what I was doing out of jail. They were turning away to keep out of direct eye contact, maybe scared of me, but glancing over to see how guilty I looked.

They were checking out this all-American suit and tie friend with me too. I did not care. There was something freeing about having your world fall apart. Free as in free-fall, just before you hit.

Don leaned forward and spoke quietly. This made everyone watch us even more. "Maybe it would be better if we went out somewhere by ourselves."

I got an espresso and a couple croissants in a plastic bag. We ended up sitting on a bench at the museum, far away from anyone except the kids doing tricks on their bicycles and skateboards nearby on the sheltered, somewhat dry ramp. Don had not gotten suspicious of them yet. I was suspicious of everyone and he would be soon.

He read out the message as I downed croissant number one. Inspector Norton was worried about me. How thoughtful. Nothing about wishing he had sprung me from jail.

Don continued while I worked on croissant number two. Norton heard I had problems and wanted to remind me to call if anyone approached me about the dead Colonel.

It was a little late for that. Everyone was involved with dead Colonel.

Don put the paper back into his pocket and gave me his summary, "Call Norton if you know anything. And have a nice day."

He shook my hand giving me that friendly, anxious-dog look that errand boys have. He probably spent most of his time helping lost Americans find their way home or, when things went wrong, holding hands with the family after some gringo dropped dead or got run over. Or shot.

It was fine with me that I was low on Norton's radar. It did not sound like he sent any DEA guys to follow me. At least I hoped he did not. They were famous for being trigger happy. But then again, maybe that's what one of the SUVs was. They looked Mexican. I don't know. Maybe Norton outsources.

I stayed sitting on the bench. There was a big flower arrangement near me, part of yet another altar. I pulled out one of the flowers. God was not looking. I did some call-Norton-yes, call-Norton-no, decision making, pulling off petals.

I ought to grease my entry back into the States and that meant calling Norton. But I wanted to lay low and that meant doing nothing. I was thinking of getting out of Oaxaca later today and buying tickets at the last minute to keep anyone from stopping me, either here or in the States. I did not want someone asking me about burning dogs and houses in LA or about dead miners in Mexico when I flew into the States. Norton could help with that. Maybe I would call. After Ruiz.

Then I would lay low the rest of the day finishing packing. Waiting for the rain to slow up. But I had to see Ruiz. There was a revolving door in the police station and Ruiz spun it to get me out; he could spin it again to put me back in.

I went home and waited. The big Mercedes picked me up just as Ruiz' man had said. The secretary was there at the office. She aimed me at a room way in the back, shooting me a minimal glance while pointing a two-inch fingernail down the hall. In the room, one wall was covered by a map with little picks and shovels drawn on it. I played it casual and did not go up close, just sat and waited. And waited. I did mental exercises to keep me from looking at the map; I did not want to know what was there. Maybe little bodies, too.

To use up time I did some visualizing. I visualized food. Today could be my last meal. Last one here in Oaxaca, I mean. I hope that's what I mean. In a couple minutes I had sauces dripping everywhere in my visions of platters full of food. I was salivating. This kept me busy. Twenty minutes went by like a first course.

Then Ruiz walked in and it all disappeared. He shook my hand. His was cold. Mine felt a little greasy. I forgot to visualize napkins.

"Señor Evans, I am sorry about the confusion. Some of my colleagues are much too zealous. We normally let investigations mature and the guilty pop out, like rats from their holes when you shoot them. And we know that you were just hungry that day. Hungry for trout. Being hungry for our Oaxacan food is normal."

Was I being called a rat? A hungry rat? One to shoot when I stuck my head out?

We sat, he in his big throne of a chair in front of the map and I on a bench. I was in a listening mood but needed to thank him first. That is what you do when you get a favor here. Maybe grovel a little. He was waiting for it.

"I must thank you for taking me from the jail. I appreciate it and hope that I can repay you some day."

He was just as polite. "You already have. Your suggestions were most helpful. I wanted to tell you earlier, but you had left for the US." He reached into the desk, pulled out a typed page and glanced at it. I think he was waiting for me to explain why I had left. I said nothing. We did a little cat and mouse. I was the quiet mouse. He was the smiling cat. Like he knew something I didn't. But everyone knew something I didn't.

"I went to a funeral in the States," I confessed. Cats always win.

"Ah, condolences to you on the loss of your wife." Of course, he knew it all, but had to let me know he knew, before we could start the real business of the day.

"We have been trying to watch out for you. We have a few men in the streets looking for criminal activity and following you when they could. You may have enemies. Many things are happening in Oaxaca right now. Many people are out and some are not good people. We try to watch out for our friends."

I guess I was happy he was my friend. That was two new friends today, if you counted Don.

"I have heard disturbing news." He looked down at the paper. "Do not worry, Señor Evans, it is not about you. It is about the mine. I have heard that the army is going to take it over very soon. That will make it very difficult for us to show to the investors if the army is there. I may ask you to come with us to talk with our investor visitors."

What could I do with the visitors? Be a shield? It looked like I was his expert again. I smiled. "I would be most happy to help."

Randy had told me it was not Ruiz' mine. It was the ex-Governor's. But it looked like Ruiz was figuring out how to do a takeover. But the ex-Governor was circling his wagons and the army was leading the way. I realized that I was starting to think like Efraím, thinking Mexican a little. No tourist thoughts any more. Just guys-with-guns thoughts.

"I will let you know when the investors arrive. I am waiting to see what happens with the army. You know the army sometimes goes too far to restore order and clean up problems. I am trying to find out more. I will wait until it is safe at the mine and call you."

That was enough for me. The army was coming. Time to do my Paul Revere and let Efraím's pueblo know what was coming. The army had machine guns mounted on pickups and God knows what else. The village had pop guns and a Volkswagen they could roll back and forth.

I got out of his office fast. I wanted to contact Efraím. His family needed to get out quick. You cannot stop armies; you can just lie low for a while. I only hoped the army would not bulldoze or burn or do whatever armies do to villages.

I took a cab to the Zocalo. No one followed me. I was going to phone Efraím from there and warn him, but from a public payphone.

I called. Efraím was out. His wife Lucia answered and said he would be back. I took another cab out to his house to wait. Lucia greeted me, surprised. I had never been there by myself. Only with Efraím. She asked me to come in and wait. I said I liked the porch, if that was OK. She shook her head and went back in.

The rain was going crazy. I watched while I was sitting on the porch, far back under the eaves, looking out. The trees by the road shook in the wind, little rivers ran down the street, and rain splashed up on the porch. What a day.

I watched the traffic on the road and thought about the pickups full of soldiers that had been riding around during the strikes, the ones that would be heading out to Efraím's pueblo soon. The soldiers always stood in the back and bounced around, holding their rifles and machine guns ready. Not quite pointed at us on the street, but not quite away from us either. Making sure we knew who was boss. That was with tourists around. If they hit the village there would be no tourists taking pictures, and no pictures in the *Sección Roja*, either. There would just be no village. Only cleaned off land and a little fortress for the ex-Governor, one Ruiz would have trouble taking over.

My mind slowed a little. Why did Ruiz tell me? I had to think this through and get it right. No Efraím was here to do it. All I could think of was the ex-Governor and his dinosaurs leading the army, ordering them to wipe out the village and take the mine. Ruiz wanted to stop them. The army would make his investors run.

Did he tell me in order to get the word back to the States, maybe for some press about the army to slow things down? Or maybe Ruiz wanted me to tell the village so they would call the Mexican press and screw up the ex-Governor's invasion plans? Or maybe he just wanted to scare everyone and free up the road for his investors that would be coming? What was it Efraím said—"of course he is lying, but which parts are lies." That was the question.

I was trying to be blank, sitting there waiting as Lucia worked away calmly in the kitchen. I calmed down a little too, but then some fireworks went off down the street, sounding like a bomb, and my mind went crazy.

My head was in another time, back in Baltimore. My father was there. He was breathing hard, standing beside me, pretty shaky. Something had happened. I was young, ten or eleven, and thought he would fix it, like they did on the TV shows. But he did not. He knew you could not fix everything. The mafia owned his job and owned him. I never knew exactly what happened. He never talked about it. But he kept his job. Everyone has their own Ruiz somewhere in their life.

But he said that I was not going to live like that. He planned my escape from a life like his. He paid my way out, for college. I left Baltimore and never went back.

Maybe that was why I was here. Looking for a place to go back to.

Lucia came out. She was staring at me when I looked up and noticed her. She had a drink for me. "To warm you," she said. I took it and my thoughts snapped back from Baltimore to Oaxaca. I thanked her in a formal Mexican way and asked about Efraím. She had no news.

She was a home-wife and did not know where Efraím went that day. I bet she seldom knew exactly where he was. Efraím led a complicated life running around in his cab. No one ever knew where he was, but you could always call him. Only not today.

His brother was gone, too. Then I noticed Efraím's cab in the back. He never went anywhere without it.

They must have him. The army or the dinosaurs or maybe Ruiz. It was up to me to tell the village. Even in this rain, in this hurricane.

I asked Lucia if she had a number for Efraím´s father. She gave it to me and I tried but the phones in the pueblo were out. That happened when it rained. Suspicious, but maybe the army was not there yet.

Then I asked the big question.

Lucia knew that Efraím and I were friends, but this was a big thing. "I need to go to his pueblo. I need to tell Efraím's father something important. I need to tell him quickly. I need to borrow Efraím's cab."

I lied. I told her Efraím said it would be OK. I knew he would never do that. She was not sure. But I told her how we had gone to the pueblo earlier, and now he wanted me to go there with a message. Finally, she gave me the keys.

I hugged her and drove out. It was muddy and slippery near the house but I got back on the road with no scrapes; I just dirtied Efraím's precious cab.

I drove fast, driving like Efraím. I shouldn't have; it was way too rainy. The hurricane had arrived with its foot of water coming down. You could not see far. When I got through Ocotlán, the city half way to the pueblo, the rain clouds hung on the mountains like an ocean fog. Paul Revere never had weather like this.

After the turnoff from the highway on to the dirt road, I turned on my headlights, honked non-stop but didn't stop driving fast while I was climbing up the mountain road. The rear end slid around on the curves. The front end too. Small landslides had fallen on the roadway and I plowed into them, throwing mud everywhere. Streams ran down the road. I splashed through, praying no potholes were waiting to snap the front suspension. Nothing slowed me.

It went on this way for a while.

Then I noticed the car below. I could see the road one curve back and in a break in the low clouds as the road did a hairpin, I saw the black SUV coming up, charging up, a couple minutes behind me.

My foot got really heavy on the accelerator after that. It was easy to go fast. I was scared. The edge of the mountain, the drop, did not seem so bad anymore. The SUV did.

I pushed it for ten minutes. I think I got a little ahead. I did not see him. The SUV must have been playing it safer on the road than I was.

Then, I heard a whump-whump hitting the back of the cab. Like the one the other day. Bullets, but big ones this time. I ducked as though the cab's sheet metal doors would stop a bullet. They were shooting with something high caliber that would go through anything.

The cab slid and splashed. I kept going as fast as it would climb. Nothing important had gotten hit, at least nothing to slow me down. I felt myself to make sure I didn´t have any holes in me too.

I turned around another corner and was sheltered from the road below. It was getting foggier. And rainier. I could barely see the road. But they could not see me. That was good. The drop over the edge looked like a big white puffy cushion, like a pillow to catch you if you fell. Nice and soft. But I couldn't look there.

I forced myself to think of nothing but the road, not looking up for anything. I did not flinch going over the bumps that bounced me against the car roof. I did not look over at the drop or look for the SUV. I just stared ahead at the puddles and holes and rocks that were supposed to be the road.

Then, at the edge of the visible rocks up in front, I saw a yellow caution tape in the fog. It stretched across the road from the rocks on the mountainside to a pole stuck by the drop. It was wrapped back and forth across the road forming a flimsy yellow tape blockade. The cab went through it sliding. The tape snapped and decorated the cab like some Christmas gift. Finally the cab stopped.

The road was gone up in front. Washed down the cliff into the fog. Just mud and running water, going off in a waterfall where the road used to be. I looked back. I could not see the SUV. I could not hear it. But it was there.

There was no place to drive the cab. Just a niche on the side by the landslide, behind a big rock jutting out.

I did not think hard, I did not think at all. I just put the cab in gear, wedged my big American shoe down on the pedal, slid my foot out, struggling a second with the tight laces, leaving the shoe and throwing myself out the open car door into the rain.

I slipped in the mud as I came out the car door and kneeled there watching the caution tape streaming behind the cab like some unlucky piñata that had just gotten its final whack. The cab went gently over the edge and dropped out of sight. I was alone.

I crawled to the side of the hill. All the caution tapes were down with the cab. You could just see it from the edge, lying upside down on a ledge, not far below.

I crawled back. I was shaking and could not stand. I got to the side of the mountain and held on to the rocks.

I could only think of the SUV. I wanted it to go over the edge too, and follow the cab down the cliff. I wanted it bad. I wanted to get rid of them all with their guns and their suits, never seeing what happened out their dark SUV windows. I was plotting to kill, plotting them dead. I trembled with hope as I heard the SUV approach.

It flew past, right over the edge. It flew down a little, through the air, over where the cab had dropped. The SUV was airborne and starting to rotate, end over end, with the rear rising like some slow-motion gymnast. It went over Efraím´s cab. Then the SUV disappeared like a plane taking off on a foggy day.

It must have hit bottom, far below, but I could not hear anything, only the rain's constant beating, driving hard into the rocks and mud. Splashing down on me lying on the edge of the road.

Beans and Tortillas

There is a happy ending. At least for most of us. I am happy. It has been a month and I am still in Oaxaca. Alive. I have my espresso, my walks. And no one is following me. I did not buy that plane ticket. It was too rainy to fly out anyway.

I was a mess the day it happened though. I crawled along what was left of the road ledge beyond the washout after the SUV went past. It was not far to Efraím's pueblo. They knew me and wrapped me in blankets and dried me. I was lucky that it was a warm rain. I was OK in a couple hours.

Then they fed me beans and tortillas. My first meal.

Most of the village men were in Oaxaca and cut off from the pueblo. The ones that were left up there stood around with guns. I stayed with them.

I warned them. They said who will be crazy enough to drive here in the rain. The army? Never. They do not want their big pickups to get stuck in the mud.

So much for my Paul Revere ride in Oaxaca. I did not save anyone.

The city made up a story about me and my ride. Santo Gordo was taking something to the village. Something important. Maybe medicine. Maybe for a sick baby. Why else would he be out in the hurricane on the impossible road. No one would be so stupid as to go out without a life-or-death reason.

The ex-Governor's dinosaurs are around, but they are lying low. No one mentions the taxi's bullet holes, not the cops, not Ruiz, not the newspapers. Everyone is still trying to forget the ex-Governor. They forgot his two dead henchmen, the ones pulled up from the wrecked SUV. I don't know why those two chased me that day, probably some rumor Ruiz started to scare them. Who knows?

I hope everyone thinks that the two dead dinosaurs were just stupid like me, going out in the hurricane. Not bumped off by some gringo.

Everyone smiles now when I walk by, knowing that they have the true story about Santo Gordo. Of course, I cannot talk about it. At least I try not to. I have learned silence. Efraím keeps teaching me.

The men from the Efraím's pueblo were in Oaxaca on the day when it happened. Efraím was with them. He was leading them. It turns out they elected him head of the pueblo. They had all driven off together to meet with Ruiz downtown. That was why the cab was all alone that day.

The men were making a deal with Ruiz, and with the other village and with everyone else, except not with the ex-Governor and his dinosaurs. A deal for the gold.

Efraím thinks Ruiz told me about the Army, trying to put pressure on the villagers by getting a rumor going. To get them to sign the contract. That was why Ruiz met with me. To get the rumor spread around. To get a better deal out of pueblo. Gringos are good for that. We talk a lot.

Or maybe the army was going to come and rescue the ex-Governors mine, but got stuck in the rain. I do not know. Some things are better not to know.

Efraím was not too mad about the cab. He gave it a funeral. We drank to it, its rusty body stuck in the mountain. More dirt and rock had slid down and covered most of its body when we went there to say prayers. He said he would do a pilgrimage every year in his fancy new cab. Efraím got enough money from the deal with Ruiz to buy a fleet of cabs. A cab for everyone in the pueblo if they wanted.

I am sitting in La Avenida, right now. The expats are talking to me again. "Could have happened to anyone," they said. I am not sure what they think happened. They still have the Santo Gordo picture hung by the espresso machine and do a little gringo bow to their expat saint when they feel like it. Lance wants to send my name over to the Pope. But he said I have to be dead first.

Randy is coming down before long. She wants to be here when Lupe's baby is born. The Señora has been praying for Randy. Those two will make a good team.

Randy says she has good news soon about a settlement. The doctor bought new dogs to replace the dead ones and wants to get this over with. No one knows why his house burned.

Arturo is working hard like he always does. He is the hero of this story. Keeping clean water running in Oaxaca. Or at least trying to.

For me, I keep remembering that two men died because of me. I killed them as surely as if I pulled a trigger. I am OK about it, I think.

I cannot think of any more loose ends.

Time for my espresso.

About the Author

Charles Kerns writes mystery novels about Oaxaca and California. He first visited Oaxaca thirty years ago and now is quite at home on its streets and in its restaurants.

He lives near Oakland, California and works a bit at Stanford University.

He is currently writing a new Santo Gordo mystery, *The Oaxaca Chocolate War.*

**

13445234R00129

Made in the USA
Charleston, SC
11 July 2012